Captured Image

Colin M. Andrews

Published by New Generation Publishing in 2022

First Edition

Paperback ISBN: 978-1-80369-343-9
Ebook ISBN: 978-1-80369-344-6

www.newgeneration-publishing.com

New Generation Publishing

Location of some of the streets and other venues in Exeter mentioned

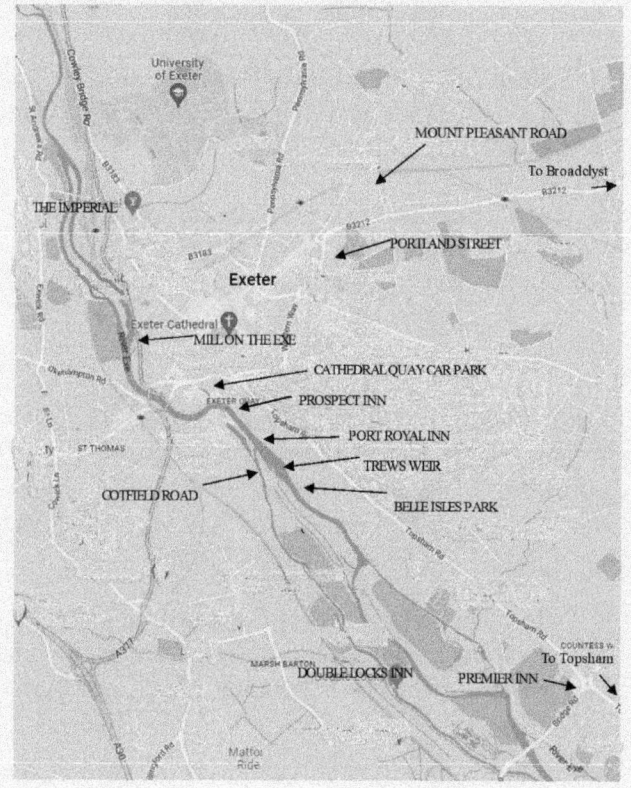

Other books by Colin Andrews

Fiction

A Matter of Degree (Matador, 2011)
Humour & drama set in teacher training college in mid-Wales in the early 1970s

Shattered Pretensions (Matador, 2015)
Two separate stories in which the actions of a young teacher have devastating consequences

One Degree Over (New Generation, 2018)
More humour and drama in the sequel to a Matter of Degree, in the year following the graduation of the main characters

Interface (New Generation, 2020)
A fast-moving thriller in which a journalist from Sydney investigates the abduction of his estranged father in London.

Poems and short stories

Who Gives A Hoot (New Generation, 2014)
A collection, mostly amusing, of original songs, parodies, poems and short stories.

Non-fiction

Shepherd of the Downs (Worthing Museum, 1979, 1987, 3rd edition self-published 2008)
The life and songs of Sussex shepherd, Michael Blann,

www.colinandrewsauthor.co.uk

PROLOGUE

All evening he'd seen her laughing, joking, flirting with other young bucks at the party, but she had given him scant attention. While he had consumed a fair amount of booze, it was nothing like the quantity she had downed. He'd noticed her top up her glass with whatever wine was available, or accept a drink from whichever male was currently chatting her up.

He had seen her beginning to look unsteady on her feet and lurch towards the stairs. She had begun to climb, awkwardly, grabbing the banister rail with both hands for support. No-one else seemed to have noticed. He had followed her, concerned that she might lose her balance and fall.

She had reached the landing. He had assumed that she was heading for the upstairs toilet – the closet on the ground floor had already become pretty disgusting with vomit and urine splashed all over the floor. But she had staggered past the loo and lunged through the door of one of the bedrooms. He had heard a clatter, obviously from colliding with some furniture and knocking something over. He had suspected that she had fallen over.

He had put his head round the door. She had collapsed onto the unmade single bed. The room had been unlit but from the landing light he had seen discarded items of clothing – socks, pants, and a T shirt – scattered on the floor by an upturned chair and tumbler. He had entered and, without thinking, closed the door behind him. The street lamp outside had still given some light into the room.

She had been lying on her back, completely out of it, eyes closed and her bosom, partially exposed by her low-cut dress, gently rising and falling with each breath. Her short skirt had risen up to her waist, revealing a skimpy pair of white lace panties that left nothing to the imagination of what lay beneath.

He had felt his erection pressing against his jeans and

a growing moistness. Some of his friends had boasted about their sexual exploits but it was something he had never experienced with another person. To avoid the embarrassment of soiling his underwear, he unwrapped a condom from the pack that had fallen next to the tumbler. Had he been sober, he would have gone no further, fully aware of the consequences if he gave in to temptation. But instead he had taken down his jeans and pants, ripped off her panties and lowered himself onto her. His fingers first had probed and then he had entered her, and ejaculated almost immediately in an explosive orgasm beyond his wildest imagination. As he had reached his climax she had emitted a soft cry and he had thought he'd seen her eyes open briefly. But she had still remained unconscious.

He'd regretted his action almost as soon as he'd withdrawn, and had seen with horror the stain of blood on the sheets and around her pubic area. He had quickly dressed again and cautiously opened the bedroom door. He had heard the sound of voices and pop music, indicating that the party was still in full swing. No-one had been in the hallway. He had crept downstairs, weighing up whether to leave immediately or rejoin the party.

Chapter 1

Malcolm Weston finally yielded to temptation.

He'd been tempted before, of course, on several occasions, but he had never quite plucked up the courage to respond to any invitation that had arrived in his inbox. He had been amazed at the number of women who had apparently been attracted by his profile on the dating website - enough in the first two weeks alone to enjoy all kinds of sexual encounters with a different partner three times a day for a year, if he'd felt so inclined. And that despite the fact that on his profile he had been completely open about his pensionable age, his bald, cadaverous appearance and his aversion to piercings, tattoos, inflated breasts and any form of kinky sex. Furthermore, he hadn't posted a photograph, for fear of being recognised by anyone who knew him as a respectable widower.

Though he had experienced a stirring in his groin on the rare occasions he had chanced across a picture of a topless young woman, Malcolm would have been horrified if anyone had suggested that he was into pornography or sexual gratification from indecent photographs. He had sought occasional self-relief in the last sexless year of his marriage but he had never contemplated infidelity and breaking his marriage vows.

Malcolm had been living alone for almost a year since Barbara, his wife, had been taken by sudden and severe return of cancer only a couple months into his retirement and soon after their silver wedding anniversary. He had been looking forward to spending some quality time with her, perhaps travelling abroad to places that they had never quite got round to visiting, even though they had never been limited by children. Barbara was unable to conceive after the birth of a daughter from her first marriage - a daughter who had long broken off any contact whatsoever with her mother, for a reason Malcolm had never fathomed and Barbara had never explained. He had no idea whether she was even aware of her mother's death

Malcolm had signed up to the Flirty website a few weeks earlier. He'd received an email with an innocuous subject heading something like 'Alone and grieving for your loved one?' Out of curiosity Malcolm had opened the email. The blurb implied that there was a good prospect of finding someone of suitable age with whom to share his advancing years. He had clicked on the link and had signed up with a pseudonym, as recommended, and a little-used email address, neither of which directly revealed his identity.

It was only when messages began arriving that he realised that the site was essentially directed towards those seeking casual sexual relationships. Most other women who had sent him invites, flirts and sex requests on the Flirty website didn't interest him at all. A few had aroused enough interest for him to click on their profile, but that was a far as he'd taken it. Until now. Malcolm was captivated by the woman on screen. Her photograph reminded him of his late wife; Barbara, in her younger days had displayed a similar delicate upturned nose, brown eyes, smooth cheeks, dark brown hair to her shoulders - and the same sardonic smile. He opened the profile of OnlyOne, as she called herself, to display her personal details and found an even more revealing picture of her body, stretched out naked upon a bed. Malcolm could hardly take his eyes off her firm rounded breasts and shaved pubic area. Barbara had never really felt comfortable in displaying her private parts to him and would certainly never have shaved herself thus.

He read what she had written about herself. OnlyOne was single, fifty years old, a non-smoker, and looking for someone to 'fill a void in her life'. Eager to respond, he began to compose a message. With only sixteen years age difference between them, Malcolm was confident that he might be in with a chance, particularly as she had made the first move, so to speak, in sending him an invite.

His hopes were nearly dashed at the first hurdle. Not

having made any responses before, he was reminded by a pop-up message that he didn't have any credits. Undeterred by the information that every message would cost nearly two pounds, Malcolm used his Paypal account to buy ten credits, the minimum purchase allowed. The amount of money some women probably spent on Flirty messaging passed briefly through his mind. Some, he had noticed, even wasted more credits in following up unanswered invitations (all, previously, in his case) with accusations of rudeness for not accepting an offer to jump into bed at the first opportunity.

With payment approved, Malcolm looked at his original message:

You are very attractive. I would very much like to meet up with you

and then added, so as to not give any false impressions:

I am 66 years old, and widowed. All fit and healthy.

He sat at his laptop for several minutes before he accepted that a swift reply was unlikely. He left the machine powered up and checked regularly during the rest of the afternoon. He found several new invites from other women but nothing from OnlyOne. He thought about sending her another message but then considered his own usual lack of action in replying to Flirty invitations that did not interest him.

Malcolm was resigned to disappointment as he prepared to close down the machine later that evening, but made one last check. OnlyOne had replied!

Your age doesn't matter to me, sweetheart. All I want is a kind man. We can meet.

Elated, he started to reply, then realised she had not given any indication of where she lived in her profile. He hoped she would not be too local but not too distant either. The next county perhaps.

I'd like that. Where do you live?

Exeter. And you?

His spirits slumped. Probably at least three hours drive even with no traffic congestion.

That's a shame. I'm in East Sussex. Sorry.

Don't give up, sweetheart. We can work something out.

Possible, Malcolm thought to himself, since I don't have any other pressing commitments here in Brighton.

I could come down for a few days

Yes!!

When would suit you?

This weekend? Please send me your photo

The only photo he knew he could find easily on the laptop was the one he had used for his driving license and passport. He had hardly changed in appearance in the two years since it had been taken, and, as such photos go, it wasn't uncomplimentary. He searched the screen for the photo upload facility.

This is me. Hope you're not put off.

Of course not, you lovely man.

Malcolm was aware that his credits were fast being gobbled up, and there was a lot more information he needed to know in order to physically meet up with OnlyOne

Low on credits. Address & phone to arrange time & place to meet.

Not comfortable with address yet. Mobile yes. Do you know Exeter?

Uni there 45 years ago.

Great. Sat 1 pm Prospect Inn on Quay. Or later?

Malcolm was familiar with the location. He added his mobile number to his reply.

1 pm fine. Will travel Fri to be sure. 1 credit left. Looking forward to meeting you. Your real name? I'm James.

He'd signed up as JamesIII. Both his father and grandfather had been called James, and it was also his middle name, so James the third seemed appropriate. It was unlikely that anyone on Flirty would make the connection.

Can't wait. Lots of love, Tricia

Next morning the elation he had felt the previous

evening had given way to anxiety. He began to wonder whether he had made a rash decision to travel a long distance to meet with a woman he didn't know - and for what? A sexual fling? Or was there really the possibility of friendship, with the prospect of intercourse as a bonus? After turning things over in his head all morning, he had more or less made up his mind, but felt the need for some reassurance.

One of Malcolm's drinking companions at their local, The Long Man of Wilmington (named after a giant carved out of the chalk hills a few miles from Brighton), had moved in to a small semi just down the road a few months ago, and they had soon established a casual friendship.

Malcolm found Barney Newton in paint-stained overalls putting finishing touches to a front window frame.

"Hi there!" he said cheerily, "be with you soon."

Inside there was ample evidence of further recent decoration in various stages of completion.

"Just put those things on the floor," said Barney as he lowered his corpulent frame into an old armchair.

Malcolm moved a baked bean tin of white spirit and used paintbrush from the wooden chair and sat down. "I'm thinking of going away for a few days, and wondered if you could feed Shylock again."

"Sure, no problem. How long are you going to be away this time?" Barney had looked after Malcolm's cat when he'd been away on some academic conference a couple of months previously.

"Um, not sure, exactly," Malcolm replied. Which was the absolute truth, since he had no idea how things would turn out when he and Tricia met up. He might find himself heading back home after just one night. On the other hand ...

"Anywhere nice?"

"Just down to Exeter."

"Have you been there before?"

"Not for quite a long time."

"Staying with a friend?"

"Possibly but otherwise I'll can use a Travelodge or Premier Inn to start with and take it from there." Malcolm paused, before raising the topic on which he really wanted another opinion. "Tell, me, do you remember friend-finding sites on the internet being mentioned at the pub a few weeks ago? To cater for lonely old widowers like us?"

Barney furrowed his brow, "Er, vaguely. Why?"

"Have you ever used one yourself?" Malcolm looked at the gold ring on Barney's finger. He'd never mentioned a wife, but whether he was divorced or widowed Malcolm didn't enquire. No doubt Barney would tell him sometime in the course of conversation.

"Not really. Had a brief look on one occasion but never took it further. I don't think any sensible woman would be interested in a fat old fart like me. Anyway I've got my niece to keep an eye on me during term time."

Malcolm thought that might explain the light red coat he had noticed hanging on the hall stand. It would never have fitted Barney.

"Now, you, you've still got a gentlemanly appearance," Barney continued. "Going to try your luck ?"

"No, just curious," Malcolm denied. Evidently though, Tricia must have seen something positive in his photograph. He decided not to pursue the matter and return to safer ground, "Anyhow, I'll let you know when I'm coming back, but if you could feed Shylock from Friday evening until Sunday morning in the first instance that would be great."

"Fancy a coffee - or a beer?"

"Thanks, but no. I've got a few things to sort out!"

Chapter 2

Although the Autumn term was well under way and families were less likely to be travelling to the West Country for their holiday, Malcolm still expected the roads to be busy. To avoid the risk of getting delayed on Saturday, even with an early start, he'd already planned to travel on Friday. He set out after breakfast, content to take a leisurely drive. Before the construction of the M27 around Southampton, and various other by-passes through towns not built with motorised traffic in mind, the journey from Brighton to Exeter would have probably been around five hours. Now it was more like three hours. He made good time, and stopped for an early lunch at a pub just after crossing the county border from Dorset into Devon.

When he'd phoned to sort out a bed for Friday evening, his college friend, Charlie, with whom he'd stayed on a previous visit was most apologetic but he expected to be out of town for a couple of days. He did consider contacting Simon or William, other pals in the area with whom he'd kept in touch over the years, but settled on using one of the budget chains. On the internet, he'd found several such hotels in Exeter, most of which had been built since his student days, and opted for one transformed into a Premier Inn, at Countess Wear, on the southern boundary of the city,

Having checked in, it was still only mid-afternoon. Malcolm toyed with the idea of contacting Tricia to suggest they could meet that same evening, but she had set the time and place presumably to suit any other commitments she may have had. He sent a brief text to her mobile,

"Now in Exeter. Meet soon. JamesIII"

A few minutes later he received a reply

"I'll be there. xxx"

Malcolm decided to stretch his legs after the long drive, and take advantage of the warm and sunny early October weather to walk to the Quay along by the canal. He remembered visiting a pub on the canal banks and wondered if it was still there. He reckoned it would take him about an hour, and if he didn't feel up to the return journey on foot, there was always the possibility of getting a bus to his hotel,

On his previous visit a few years earlier he'd not been down to the canal area. Malcolm was therefore pleasantly surprised at the changes to the Quay area since his student days. Gone was the maritime museum, occupying old warehouses on both sides of the canal. In its place were bars and eateries, a microbrewery, a large piazza and apartment blocks, all in all a very attractive setting and thoughtfully modernised. Malcolm took one of the few vacant tables outside a pizza restaurant and enjoyed a leisurely meal. It was almost dark when he arrived back at Countess Wear Premier Inn. Feeling tired after the driving and the long walk, he decided to crash out early and conserve his energy for the following evening. If all went well he might be in a different bed, possibly even sharing a bed, for the rest of the weekend.

Malcolm slept soundly. Over breakfast, he debated whether to use his free pass and catch a bus into the city, or whether to take his car into the city, to have it easily available for himself and Tricia if necessary. He reckoned that to have it reasonably on hand would be the best option. He suspected that daytime car parking would be expensive, and remembered from his student days that there was usually plenty of unlimited in street parking outside his old digs in Portland Street, even though it would take him a quarter of an hour to walk to the Quay. Exeter City Council had moved with the times, however, and Malcolm found that residents-only parking, limited waiting and parking meters seemed to be everywhere within a mile of the city centre.

With plenty of time to spare, he paid for a couple of hours in a nearby public car park and sauntered into the city centre, past the old bus station. It had altered very little in forty odd years, though it was evident some major changes were planned, with diggers and lorries in the former coach park. Across the way a modern cinema had been built on the site once occupied by a long defunct D.I.Y. chain store, while opposite the bus station all that remained of the iconic Honiton Inn was a pile of rubble The main shopping centre of High Street and Sidwell Street he also recognised quite clearly, but now augmented by a huge John Lewis store and a generic shopping mall that had replaced the quaint but dated Princesshay pedestrian precinct. He was pleased to find some of the old pubs he used to frequent as a student were still there, but of others there was no sign at all.

His morning spent at leisure, Malcolm returned to his car and drove down to a multi-storey car park near the Quay,. He arrived at the Prospect early. He hoped to catch sight of Tricia before she spotted him, and, in the unlikely event that her photograph had been over-generously kind to her appearance, he could, as a last resort, back out. He wore sunglasses and a straw hat so that she might not have the same opportunity by early recognition.

One o'clock approached with no sign of her. A woman's prerogative to be late, Malcolm rationalised. Two o'clock came and went and Tricia still had not showed up, nor anyone remotely resembling her photograph. No messages on his mobile phone. He rang her number. Her phone was switched off. Still on his own at half past two, Malcolm's emotions were oscillating between disappointment, concern about Tricia, and anger that his journey had been wasted. He looked ruefully at the photo of her he had printed out. On an impulse he entered the pub and approached the barman.

"Excuse me, I wonder if you have seen this lady in the pub today," he said, showing the barman the picture. "We had planned to meet here this lunchtime."

The barman looked closely at the photograph and frowned. "I'm not sure. I've only just come on duty. Kev might know." He called his colleague over. "Seen this woman?"

"Dunno," said Kev, "I might have seen her before."

"Today?"

"Nah, don't think so."

Malcolm was in quandary. Should he stay, on the off-chance that she might still turn up? But surely she would have sent a message? If he left, he had the rest of the afternoon and evening, to himself in all probability. Perhaps she had caught sight of him and changed her mind as he might have done had her appearance not met his expectations. He got himself a coffee and made it last another half hour. Still no sign of Tricia.

He approached Kev, the barman, once more. "Look, I had arranged to meet this person here this afternoon. She's probably been delayed but I'm not able to get in touch with her and I can't really hang around much longer. Could I leave my mobile number with you and if she does come in please let me know – I'm James – or, better, ask her to ring me?"

Kev's look suggested he was holding back from making a snide remark about an old geezer being stood up, but he took the number reluctantly. "Yeah, okay."

Malcolm had little enthusiasm for further sightseeing but sitting twiddling his thumbs and consuming more alcohol had little appeal either. He wandered along the canal bank, passing a smartened up Mill on The Exe pub, and then on to the main St. David's station. He checked his phone regularly for messages, and called Tricia's mobile several times, always with the same result. Nothing. He considered contacting Simon or William but didn't think he'd be terribly good company, even if they were around. To compound his depression he noticed that the old Jolly Porter pub, where he'd spent many a pleasant evening at the folk club in his student days, was closed or had been converted into a restaurant, even though the original pub name was still displayed.

He'd only grabbed a sandwich at lunchtime, with the expectation of dining out in a decent restaurant with Tricia in the evening. He wasn't yet over-hungry but there didn't really seem much point in returning to the Prospect, and he didn't fancy the Beefeater at the Premier Inn. Many tables had been spread out in the grounds of the Imperial Hotel, which he he'd noted on his previous visit had undergone a Wetherspoon's conversion. It was moderately busy but no doubt in another couple of hours it would be heaving with students from the nearby halls of residence. Malcolm had a table to himself and mulled over his options. Basically, there were just two; stay another night or two in Exeter and hope to re-establish contact with Tricia by phone or the Flirty site, or go home.

Reluctantly he decided that to head back home next morning after breakfast made the most sense.

His mobile pinged with an incoming message.

Sorry. Emergency. Please forgive me. Can make 8.30 pm xxx Tricia

His spirits rose. He quickly thumbed a reply.

Great. Want to see you. Same place? Xxx Malcolm.

Prefer Port Royal. Ok?

Malcolm would have preferred the original pub. The new venue was a few minutes walk by a footpath and cycle track further along the canal. But he replied,

Ok. I'll be there.

He was just about to put his phone back in his pocket when it rang again on normal voice call. "Charlie? I thought you were away."

"I was. Just got home. I've only just picked up your message. You're in Exeter for a meeting?"

"Yes. It was supposed to be at one o'clock at The Prospect but I've literally just heard it's been rescheduled for 8.30 this evening at the Port Royal."

"Sounds more like pleasure than a business meeting then."

"Now that would be telling!"

"Sorry I couldn't help with giving you somewhere to kip."

"No problem, I've booked into the Countess Wear for

two nights."

"Keep in touch. See you sometime."

His food arrived. He still had a couple of hours or so to kill before his rendezvous, so he took his time over his lasagne. He refrained from topping up with another pint, conscious of the fact that he would be driving again later, either back to his hotel or to wherever Tricia may have in mind.

He sauntered down towards the Quay, calling at the car park on the way to collect a coat. The evening was beginning to feel a little chilly. Evening business in the other bars and restaurants around the Quay was already quite brisk with mainly a young clientele. The Port Royal was also quite busy though very much on its own. Though there were a few other people outside, Malcolm felt a little out of place as a lone elderly gent, sitting at a table sipping a lime and soda.

By nine o'clock he was still a lone elderly gent, getting increasingly frustrated and angry. No unaccompanied woman of any age had come into the pub. He tried her mobile. Number unavailable Even if she did show up Malcolm now felt he would have difficulty in greeting her with any passion. By nine-thirty after two more unsuccessful phone calls and with his glass empty, he gave up. He looked in forlorn hope along the path that led to a footbridge over the river, close to a weir, in a last hope that she would appear from the shadows. Dejected, he retraced his steps back to his car. Almost on automatic he drove to Countess Wear, with little awareness of the route he was taking, as he turned over the events or, rather, non-events of the day in his head.

He flung his coat onto the bed. He was too worked up to expect to sleep if he went to bed. He pulled out from the bedside cabinet the bottle of Scotch he'd purchased the previous day and turned on his laptop. There were no new messages from Tricia on Flirty - not that he was now expecting any - but several from other young women offering themselves to any male who cared to respond.

One message caught his eye. Calling herself PayGal, the photograph showed a woman much the same age as himself. Malcolm fleetingly wondered whether she needed to pay men to have sex with her; he couldn't imagine any man paying her, like a prostitute. Her message sounded as if she was into the kinky sex of a dominatrix.

He switched off and stowed the laptop back in his travel case.

Chapter 3

Malcolm was woken up by his mobile ringing. Unlike the previous night, he'd not slept well, even when he'd crawled into bed around midnight, after rousing from a doze slumped over his laptop. He'd tossed and turned, and had only dropped off into a steady slumber just as dawn was breaking.

His eyebrows - and his hopes - rose when he saw the caller's number displayed.

"Tricia? Tricia, is that you?"

A pause, before a male voice answered. "Am I speaking to James?"

Confused, Malcolm started to reply, "No, I'm ..." then gathered his wits, "Yes, James speaking. Who are you?"

"I'm Detective Inspector Desmond Matthews. I would like to speak with you, as you may be able to help us."

"Help in what way?"

"We are investigating the death of an unidentified woman ...."

"Not Tricia!"

"We don't know. Look, I think it's best if we meet and talk further. May I ask where you are? We could, of course, trace your mobile but I'm sure you'd like to save us the trouble."

"I'm staying at the Premier Inn, Countess Wear. I'm intending to drive back home this morning."

"Okay, but please don't leave until we have spoken to you. We will see you there in twenty minutes."

"I've only just got out of bed. I'm not going anywhere until I've dressed and had breakfast!"

Malcolm looked at his watch. 8.30 am. He had overslept. He quickly showered and dressed, and had just seated himself at a table in the dining room when a tall, sandy-haired, middle-aged man in a suit appeared in doorway, looking round. Behind him stood a younger chap with close-cropped black hair. He would not have looked out of place in the front row of a rugby scrum.

The senior man walked over to Malcolm's table. "James?" he asked.

Malcolm nodded.

"Strange there is no record of anyone with Christian or surname of James signed in as a guest."

"That's because I'm signed in as Malcolm Weston. My middle name is James." He thought for a moment. "How did you recognise me? I presume you are D.I. Matthews."

"Yes, and this is Sergeant Nicholls." They held out I.D. cards for Malcolm to inspect. "Your photograph, mobile number and a exchange of messages were on a mobile phone we found near to the river."

"That would be Tricia's phone then." Malcolm thought for a moment before adding, "But surely if she lost it she would go to the police station herself to see if it had been handed in?"

"We've had no such enquiries. However, the body of a woman of mature years was also recovered from the river close by."

Malcolm recognised the euphemism for elderly. "But that can't be Tricia!"

"What makes you so sure?" This from the sergeant.

"Well …" Malcolm realised he hadn't actually seen her in the flesh, so to speak. "She isn't old. You surely can see from this photograph she sent that it can't be the same person." He showed him the picture that he'd already presented to the barmen at the pub.

"I'm afraid it's not quite so easy as that, sir. The woman's face was battered beyond all recognition. This is a murder investigation and so far the discovery of the phone is our only probable link to her identity."

"I see," said Malcolm. He'd lost his appetite. "Though if the phone wasn't actually found with this woman it could be pure coincidence that Tricia dropped it by accident. It would explain why she didn't return my calls."

"Ye..es, possible," conceded D.I. Matthews, "but we tend to be very suspicious of such coincidences." He looked around. The breakfast room had become quite busy. "Is there somewhere more private that we can continue this conversation? Your room, perhaps?"

"I'm happy to continue here, but okay, if you prefer. It's not very tidy. I haven't got round to packing yet."

The two detectives exchanged an unspoken message in their facial expression. "Lead the way."

Malcolm perched on the bed while the senior detective took the only chair in the room's furniture. His colleague seemed particularly interested in the jumble of discarded clothing by the small wardrobe.

"Can you tell us a bit more about this Tricia with whom you seem to have a strong phone connection?"

"She's an … um … an old friend I had arranged to meet in Exeter."

"Are you sure about that? Why then would you need her photograph?"

Malcolm closed his eyes and took a deep breath. "Yes, you're right. I lost my wife a year ago. Tricia is a person I'd arranged to meet through a dating website. She would have known me as James from that site. She didn't turn up."

"Where and when were you supposed to meet?"

"Yesterday, at the Prospect Inn on the Quay, at one o'clock. I waited until nearly three o'clock and tried contacting her several times. Her phone was off. I even showed her picture to the barmen but they couldn't confirm that she'd been there or even if they recognised her. You can check."

"Yes, we will do that."

"I'd given up, and then got another message from her, at, oh, sometime after five o'clock."

"What did it say?"

"Something had cropped up and she wasn't able to make the lunchtime meeting, but wanted to reschedule for eight thirty."

"And you agreed?"

"Of course, why wouldn't I?"

"And this new meeting, was it at the same place?

"No, the Port Royal. Are you finished now? I really need to pack and be on my way."

Inspector Matthews grimaced. "I would prefer that you stayed here in Exeter for a little longer. We may have some more questions for you when we have established an identity for the victim, Tricia, or otherwise. We would also like you to come to the police station and make a formal statement. Is that alright?"

Malcolm shrugged, "I don't suppose I've got a choice, have I? Is that the Heavitree Road station?"

"No, we've moved out to new premises by the County Police HQ."

"Oh, at Middlemoor, you mean?"

"Yes. You seem to know Exeter quite well."

"I was at university here but I've only been back on odd occasions since then, and not for three for four years at least."

"So where do you live now," the sergeant asked.

"Brighton. Have done for many years. I was a lecturer at Sussex University until I retired last year."

"Why did you come all the way to Exeter, then, for a blind date?"

"I saw this person on the website who reminded me of my late wife. I asked to meet her and she agreed."

Inspector Matthews didn't look convinced. He stood up. "Just one more question. Can you tell us where you were yesterday evening between, say seven o'clock and midnight?"

"I had an early supper at the Imperial. I was there until sometime after seven. I walked back to my car in the multi-storey nearest the Quay, and then to the Port Royal. Got there some time after eight o'clock and left about nine thirty - by which time I was rather pissed off. Again she didn't show up."

"Did anyone see you? Can anyone back up your account?"

"Well, I did pass a few other people on my walk but I doubt if they would remember me any more than I'd remember them. I did use my card to pay at the Imperial so there will be a record of that."

"How about at the Port Royal?

"I only had a glass of lime and soda. Paid cash. I was driving and I'd already had a couple of beers during the day. They were busy but the barman might remember me.

Nicholls glanced at the half empty whiskey bottle. "Looks as if you made up for it."

"I was pissed off, and then got well and truly pissed, you might say."

"Did you speak to anyone when you got back here? The person on duty at the desk, perhaps?"

"No, sorry."

"Okay, thank you for your co-operation. Could you please come to Middlemoor at, say, three pm. to make a formal statement?"

Malcolm nodded. When they had departed he sat on the bed with his head in his arms. He wished he'd never got involved with the Flirty site. He'd have to ask Barney to feed Shylock for another night and check that this room would be available. He might also try contacting his old friends again. He wasn't enjoying his own company in the present circumstances.

In their car, as D.I. Matthews secured his passenger seatbelt, he asked his sergeant, "What was your impression of Weston, Bob?"

"I'm not sure, sir," he replied, "He seemed pretty straightforward and honest but there are some things that just don't add up."

"I'm inclined to agree. He's got no alibi. He's got a possible motive if the dead woman is Tricia and she stood him up. I take it you didn't notice any bloodstained clothing?"

"No such luck!"

When they got back to their station they found the pathologist's report awaiting their attention. Inspector Matthews had asked for the examination to be expedited in the hope that it would reveal some clue to the woman's identity.

He skimmed through the pages. "Confirmation that she was about sixty years old, and in reasonably good health for her age. No sign of sexual assault. Oh, that's interesting!"

Nicholls raised his eyebrows.

"It is likely that the severe injuries to her face were inflicted post-mortem - probably shortly after she died." said his boss.

"That might explain why we didn't find a lot of blood around the crime scene - and Mr Weston might not have got bloodstains on his clothes. If he did it, of course."

"Good point, Bob. We also have a time of death estimated at somewhere between nine pm and midnight."

"Could she have been killed elsewhere then dumped in the river?"

"Possibly, but the report suggests death, battering, and immersion in water were within the same time frame." He scratched his head. "Still nothing to tell us who she was. We could check dental records but it would be helpful to know whether she was even local."

The telephone rang. The sergeant picked up the receiver and listened, making a few notes on a pad. "We may have a murder weapon - or rather, a weapon used to inflict the damage to her face."

Matthews raised his eyebrows. "And?"

"A fisherman found a hammer by the riverside not too far from where the body was recovered. It's been sent to forensics to see if they can find any blood traces or, if we're very lucky, fingerprints."

"We may also be able match the hammer to the wounds" Matthews mused. "I'll get onto the pathologist." He was reaching for the handset which his sergeant had only just replaced when the phone rang again.

"Matthews here." He listened to the caller for a few moments before responding. "Did you take a contact number or address?" Short pause then, "Brilliant, we're on our way." He put the phone down. "Some bloke has just reported his wife missing. May be the breakthrough we need."

Chapter 4

Frank Gallagher lived in a small terraced house in Cotfield Street. Parking was at a premium but Sergeant Nicholls squeezed the car into a small gap between an old VW Polo and a well-used pickup bearing the sign, 'F. Gallagher, General Builder'.

The knock on the door was answered by a thick-set man about six feet in height. His thinning grey hair was long and unkempt, and a large veined broken nose stood out from his stubbled face. A muscular arm propped open the door, all the tattoos on his arms and neck fully exposed by the grey sleeveless vest he wore.

Matthews introduced himself and his sergeant. "Mr Gallagher?"

"Have you found her?" A surprisingly high pitched voice, with a trace of an Irish accent.

"Possibly, sir. May we come in?"

Gallagher stood back and waved them in to the living room, which was compact but tidy. They took the couple of hard back chairs while their host slumped down onto a sofa that had seen better days.

"Mr. Gallagher, we are investigating the death of an as yet unidentified woman whose body was found in the river."

He screwed up his eyes and lowered his head. "You think it's her?"

"We don't know yet. When did you last see … your wife? Her name?"

"Patty. Early Saturday morning I had a job to finish off and then went to see the Grecians play. Slipped out of the top three again - we missed a penalty and then beaten by stupid goal! Went with my mates for a bite to eat afterwards. She wasn't here when I got home."

"What time was that?"

"Well after dark, so probably at least eight-thirty."

"Were you surprised not to find your wife at home?"

"No, not really, She goes to a couple of craft clubs, and sometimes stays overnight with a friend in Topsham. But when she hadn't come back by late this morning I was getting a bit concerned. She's quite traditional in cooking a roast for Sunday. I couldn't get any reply on her mobile, and when I rang her friend, she hadn't been there last night."

"What kind of mobile did she have?"

"Oh it was an old Nokia. You could make phone calls, send texts and take photos but not all the fancy things that these smartass phones can do."

That was not the phone they had discovered.

"So you were expecting her to be back before lunchtime?" asked Bob Nicholls

"Yes. Only a couple of times has she been away for a night and that's never happened at a weekend."

"Any reason for these longer absences?"

Frank paused before replying. "If we've had an argument."

"And had you? On Saturday?"

"No, not really. Well, I'd called her a silly cow - she'd left the light on in the bathroom all night, and insisted I'd done it. But we didn't argue because I'd left for work straight afterwards."

Matthews thought for a moment before putting the next question. "I'm sorry to raise this matter, but have you ever had any reason to believe she might be seeing another man?"

Frank's eyes narrowed and his face flushed. "She wouldn't bloody dare!" he growled. He quickly realised that his reply didn't reflect well on him, and said in a calmer voice, "What makes you suggest that?"

"Just covering various angles. Truth is, we don't know yet whether your wife is the victim. By the way, have you got a recent photograph of Patty? It might help us."

Frank pointed to a couple of framed photographs on the mantelpiece. "They were taken last year."

One was not any use, since both the woman and the man, almost certainly Frank, were wearing sunglasses and large straw hat. The other showed a mature women in a summer dress smiling at the camera, against a background of a beach which Matthews recognised as Teignmouth.

"That's Patty," Frank said.

Buxom, and shorter than her husband by a few inches, she still showed a reasonably good figure for her age, though slightly overweight. The smile looked genuine and her face was relatively free of wrinkles – possibly due to make-up, but difficult to tell from the photo.

"May we borrow this?" Matthews asked. "Also, if you have a hairbrush your wife used, we should be able to extract some DNA that will enable us to identify whether the body is that of your wife."

Frank nodded. "Can I see her?"

"That's probably not a good idea at the moment, until we know for certain at least. Our victim suffered some significant injuries to her face."

Frank grimaced. "Excuse me for a moment." He went upstairs and soon returned with a hairbrush and a scent bottle, "You'll find her fingerprints on this bottle, no doubt"

"Thank you. In which case, if we could borrow a teacup or glass you've recently handled, we'll be able to eliminate your prints!" Both officers stood up ready to leave. "Just one more question, could you tell us whether you went out again on Saturday evening?"

"No, I was here watching television until I went to bed."

"Thank you for your time. We'll be in touch as soon as we have any news one way or the other.

Outside, Matthews looked at his watch. "Any thoughts?"

"He's another possible suspect, sir. No alibi. And if he did suspect his wife was seeing someone else, he'd have a motive."

"Look him up on the files. See if he's got previous form."

"Pity the mobile we found isn't hers."

"Oh come on, Bob! Would you keep private messages to a lover on a phone your wife had access to?"

"Suppose not." Nicholls paused then added, "I'm

wondering, sir, whether it might be a good idea to put off the formal statement from Weston until tomorrow. We may well know by then the identity of the victim and possibly have some prints from the hammer."

"Good thinking, Bob. We might even get what's left of Sunday with our families!"

Chapter 5

Malcolm knew that Charlie Coombes was back home, but he also had phone numbers for Simon Cook and William Forth, his other two former student flatmates who were still in the Exeter area. William, a recently retired vicar, would most likely be busy on a Sunday acting as a locum, or whatever such term applied to the clergy.

"Simon Cook speaking."

Malcolm recognised immediately the strong Scouse accent. Simon had never moved back to Liverpool.

"Hi, Simon, it's Malcolm - Malcolm Weston."

"Malcolm! How are you doing?"

"I had to come down to Exeter yesterday for a meeting. Anyhow, I've got a bit of free time and wondered whether you'd like to meet up for a drink. I'll probably be heading back home tomorrow."

"Er, yes, delighted! I was intending to go out this afternoon but either lunchtime or this evening would be good. Pity you didn't let me know earlier - you would have been welcome to stay here."

"Thanks, but it was a rather last minute thing. I've also got something else on this afternoon and I'm not exactly sure when I'll be free, so lunchtime would be best. Where do you suggest?"

"If you've got transport, my local, the Red Lion, would be convenient. Did you know I'd moved out to Broadclyst?"

"Yes, Great, see you then."

Although he was still very disappointed that the purpose of his visit to Exeter had been come to nothing, he felt at little more at ease now he'd some social contact arranged. He had also made arrangements for a further night's accommodation and the feeding of his cat.

His journey to Broadclyst, on the Eastern side of Exeter, was straightforward, particularly as on a Sunday there was little traffic around the Sowton commercial estate, and the flow of vehicles from the M5 into the service area was also quite light. Malcolm was amazed, and indeed rather disapproving of the large scale commercial and residential development on what had once been green fields between the A30 at Sowton and the village of Broadclyst.Though it, too, had seen encroachment of new housing, it still retained a quiet rural atmosphere, and the Red Lion, set back from the main road through the village, looked just the sort of place you might come across morris dancers performing their capers.

Simon was already sitting at one of the tables outside, sipping a pint. He had put on a lot of weight since he had been the best man at Malcolm and Barbara's wedding over twenty five years ago, and even since her funeral his once blond full head of hair had now all turned grey. His round face was still as florid and full of good cheer as ever.

"Malcolm! What can I get you?"

"I'll have the same as you, thanks."

"Eating? I can recommend their Sunday roast."

"Yes, that's fine, thanks."

Simon returned with another pint, and cutlery for their meal. "So what brings you back to Exeter?"

"I'd arranged a meeting but the other person withdrew at short notice," Malcolm replied, keeping broadly to the truth.

"Oh that's a shame, a wasted journey."

"Well, not quite. It's an opportunity to meet you. I could have returned home straight away but opted to stay over another night on the off chance I might be able to rearrange the meeting. Not going to happen, though, as far as I can see."

You're still in the same house in Brighton?""

"Same house I was in for most of my working life. And you? A recent move I believe."

"Yes I've not fully retired yet. I still go into the office two or three days a week, and my partners know I'm just a phone call away if anything urgent crops up that they can't handle. I moved to a small cottage just down the road there." He pointed to a lane leading off the other side of the B road through the village. "You know I was divorced some time ago, so I don't need a big place, and I've got a garden to keep me busy when I'm sorting out other people's marriage break-ups or whatever.

Malcolm vaguely remembered his wife.

"Do you keep in touch with any other of our student circle, apart from Charlie and William, that is?"

"A bit. Much on the same level as with you, I suppose, as they spread out all over the country and all over the globe, most likely. I come across Charlie from time to time. He's now Editor of our local rag. The paper has been his life. He could retire on a good pension but I don't think he's got any other interests."

"I did speak to him yesterday, briefly, but I know he's been away."

"You can always try Charlie at his office. Practically lives there! You know that William is now living in Topsham?"

"Really? I knew he'd moved back this way. If he's still using the same mobile I could have called him on Friday evening, had I known."

"I'm not sure, but I'll give you his landline as well just in case." Simon pulled out his phone and scrolled through the contacts. He scribbled a number on the back of one of his business cards and handed it to Malcolm

A young chap brought out their lunch - plates well stacked with roast beef, a huge Yorkshire pudding, and all the vegetables and trimmings. They tucked in and chatted and reminisced about past shared experiences. Until Malcolm's phone rang.

"Well I suppose so. Can you make it earlier? I'd like to be on the road by midday."

Simon raised his eyebrows enquiringly.

"Ruddy police. They wanted to take a formal statement from me this afternoon but have postponed it until eleven o'clock tomorrow morning."

"Oh, why's that?" Simon said with concern.

"Nothing to worry about. They found a mobile phone

29

with my number on it near the body of an old woman down by the river. They are trying to trace its owner."

Simon wrinkled his brow. "Mmm, sounds odd. Look, I don't know quite what's going on, but it might be a good idea for me to be around in case they start regarding you as a suspect to any foul play."

"You're not serious?" Malcolm said, surprised, "I've not done anything !"

"I'm not implying you have but, believe me, I've a lot of experience in knowing how their minds work when investigating a suspicious death. I assume they are regarding the woman's death as suspicious?"

"Yes, she was battered to death."

"I'm definitely going to be on hand," said Simon "in case you need a lawyer."

"Thanks very much, Simon," said Malcolm, "I hope it can all be sorted quickly without involving you, but it's reassuring to know I can call on you."

They passed on a dessert but ordered a coffee.

"What are you going to do with the rest of the day?" Simon asked.

"Not sure. I might see if William is around."

"Okay, I'm sure he'll be up for a chat. I've got to be off shortly for another engagement, but I'll meet you at Middlemoor car park tomorrow at eleven o'clock."

Fortunately Malcolm had been able to keep the same room for another night. He'd come prepared to spend four nights away if things had worked out in his favour, but he hadn't been really been expecting more than two nights at the most in the Premier Inn.

Now in possession of William's home number, he gave his friend a call.

Chapter 6

Uncertain of whether he might consume more alcohol during the rest of the afternoon and evening, and also aware that parking could be a problem, Malcolm decided to leave his car at Countess Wear and get the bus down to Topsham. William had given Malcolm his address, a flat in the main street, virtually opposite the bus stop.

"Pleased to see you, Malcolm. Welcome to my humble abode, come on in," William stood aside to let Malcolm enter. "Up the stairs."

The flat was very compact; a lounge diner with a kitchen unit, a small bathroom with a shower, one bedroom, and a smaller room that could be used as an office, or at a pinch another single bedroom. It was currently stacked with cardboard boxes.

"Take a seat! Oh just move my dog collar onto the table." Even at university William had always shunned any formal attire like a jacket and tie, so it was no surprise that he'd discarded his symbol of holy orders in the comfort of his home. "Tea? Coffee?"

"Coffee's fine, thanks." Malcolm lowered himself into a chintzy armchair that had seen better days, while his host busied himself with the percolator. His lanky six-foot frame had developed a slight stoop with age but he was still as thin as ever. His former blonde locks which had flowed down to his shoulders were now reduced to a fringe of grey hair around a bald pate but his bright blue eyes, unhindered by spectacles, still retained a twinkle and his friendly lop-sided smile would no doubt captivate members of his congregation as it had the female students long ago.

"Well, to what do we owe this surprise?" said William, placing a steaming mug of coffee on a beer mat next to his collar.

"Long story, but the essence is that I came down to Exeter to meet someone who didn't turn up. So I have some unexpected free time."

"Was that someone female?"

"Yes, as a matter of fact. What made you think that?

"Intuition gained from experience I suppose. You'd be surprised what things I've heard in confidence in confessionals."

"I thought confessionals were a Roman Catholic thing."

"Yes, it's certainly more common with them but it does also happen from time to time in Anglican churches."

"You can take this as a confessional, if you like. It's not something I'm broadcasting to all and sundry. It was a sort of blind date."

"Have you got a photo? Just a possibility I may have come across her."

"I think that's unlikely," Malcolm fumbled into his pocket and produced a photo. "but here, have a look. Her name's Tricia."

William studied the photo and frowned, "Don't know her. But she reminds me a bit of your late wife, you know, when we met at your wedding."

"Strange you should say that, I thought the same."

"So how did you meet up?"

"We've only been in touch over the internet, so I've never actually met her in person.

"Oh, I see." William didn't feel it would be prudent to probe further into his friend's affairs, and changed the subject, "What do you think of Exeter these days? It's changed quite a bit over the years. I was quite surprised when I moved back here."

"Well, the Quay area is a definite plus but I'm not sure about the city centre developments. Hell of a lot of new student accommodation as well. What persuaded you to return?"

"You may not know, but when you retire as a vicar, you are not supposed to continue living in the parish. After a lifetime in and around the Midlands I thought it would be pleasant to be closer to the coast. This place is temporary until I can find a small place of my own. Downside, of course, is that property is not cheap around here."

"You still keep up your calling though.?"

"Oh yes, there's always plenty of demand for retired clerics like me to stand in for the incumbents particularly these days when a vicar may have to cover several parish churches. Suits me fine, I can get to know people without having quite the responsibilities and commitments of a full time post."

"How far away do you go?"

"Mostly it's pretty local – Exeter down the estuary to Exmouth and some of the nearby villages in East Devon."

"Simon mentioned that he kept in contact with you,"

"From time to time, more ad hoc than any regular event. By the way, I did let you know that Richard Eastman had died ? "

"Yes, committed suicide, I believe."

"Indeed. You know Charlie and I shared a house with him - that was before we teamed up with you and Simon. I'm not sure how he tracked me down but I had an email from him out of the blue earlier in the year."

"What did he want?"

"Difficult to say, exactly. I got the impression he felt he was not long for this world anyway and wanted to put things straight before he died. Quite sad really, but I couldn't see that I could help. His son had also found my email contact, presumably from his father, and informed me of his death. He was also trying to contact others that knew his father at university, and I said I'd pass the message on. He also was asking about the girl his father was accused of assaulting."

"Why would he want to do that?"

"Apologise to his father's victim, I suppose, though I'm doubtful whether it would be a good idea reviving bad memories after such a long time."

"I think you're right."

"Anyhow, enough of the past. Are you doing anything this evening?"

"Nothing planned," said Malcolm. "Why?"

"If you're interested the local folk club have got a concert on this evening in the hall just across the road. I haven't got tickets but there's a good chance we can get them on the door."

"Fine with me. Beats sitting around in a hotel room watching TV."

"Stay and have some supper with me first."

Chapter 7

They had already been working at their desks for an hour or so on Monday morning when they got the call they wanted. Matthews snatched up the receiver, listened to the message, and hung up.

"We've got confirmation that the body is that of Patty Gallagher. DNA match - which also matches the blood on the hammer."

"That's good, sir. Wonder if the hammer belongs to her husband? He's a builder. Apparently he has been reported on a few occasions for assaulting his wife. No charges ever brought, though." Nicholls said then added, "Any fingerprints?"

"Yes, more than one set."

"Weston's or Gallagher's?"

"We haven't got Weston's yet. They could be Gallagher's. We should know soon. But it may not be quite so straightforward."

"What do you mean, sir?"

"There is now confirmation the facial injuries were inflicted very soon after she died." said his boss.

"That's weird."

"Let's see if we can get Gallagher on his mobile. He's probably out working somewhere. We at least need to break the news to him."

*****

Malcolm arrived at Middlemoor Police Station with about ten minutes to spare. Simon was already waiting for him in the car park. "All ready? Did you get a good night's sleep." he greeted his friend.

"Not really. Just want to get this sorted and get home."

"Okay. I'm going to stay here in my car. Don't say any more than necessary to answer a question and if you are in any doubt, or they issue a caution, just ask for me and shut up until I'm with you."

Malcolm entered the station and gave the reason for his visit. He waited while the desk sergeant made a phone call. "Please take a seat, Inspector Matthews will be with you shortly."

A few minutes later the younger of the two who had spoken to him the previous day led him to an interview room where D.I. Matthews was already seated behind a desk.

"Thank you for coming, Mr Weston. We'd like you to go through what you told us yesterday, for a formal statement. We will be recording this conversation. Is that okay with you?"

Malcolm though it would make very little difference if he objected. He'd nothing to hide, so just said, "No problem. By the way, it's Doctor Weston."

"Thank you, Dr Weston. Now, first of all we'd like you to go through your activities from the time you arrived in Exeter on Friday until we woke you up with our phone call yesterday morning. Any precise times you can give would be most helpful.

Malcolm gave a full account as requested, which took nearly fifteen minutes with the detectives asking the odd question for clarification.

"Thank you. Now regarding the woman you know as Tricia and whose mobile we have found, what can you tell us about your relationship with her?"

Malcolm shrugged. "Well, there wasn't actually any relationship at all, other than the exchange of messages over the internet. I never met her in person. That was the object of my journey to Exeter."

"Remind us how you came in contact with her in the first place."

"As I said earlier, it was through a dating site called Flirty."

"Are you a regular user of this site?" asked Matthews.

"I'd never heard of it until a few weeks ago. An unsolicited email drew my attention to it."

"I bet it did," Nicholls sniggered.

Malcolm turned to him and retorted brusquely, "Just because I lost my wife a year ago doesn't mean that I lost all interest in the opposite sex!"

"Okay, okay, calm down, sir," said the Inspector, "But what made you particularly interested in this Tricia?"

"She's the only one I have ever responded to," said Malcolm, "because her appearance reminded me of my late wife."

Matthews handed over the photograph of Patty Gallagher. "Do you recognise this woman?"

Malcolm took at the photo, shook his head, then just as he was about to hand it backed, he looked again, with furrowed brows. "No, I don't know her."

"Are you sure? You seemed to show some recognition."

"It vaguely reminded me of someone I knew some forty odd years ago but haven't seen since. I doubt it's the same person. Does she have a name?"

"Patty Gallagher."

Something in the name started wheels turning in his head, but he just replied, "Never heard of her. It's definitely not the same person as the photo of Tricia I showed you yesterday."

Similar wheels had obviously been turning in Matthews' brain. "Patty - Patricia - Tricia ? Does it make you wonder whether there is a link? And I can confirm that we found Patty's fingerprints on this phone."

Malcolm gaped open-mouthed at the two detectives. "Yes, I had made that connection too, but I don't understand this at all. You can see that the photograph of Tricia I showed you is very different to the photo of Patty."

"We don't understand it either at the moment, but I assure you that we won't stop until we come up with the answer. To be honest, you could have got that photo from anywhere."

"She sent me the photo. It's all on my laptop, and all of the messages, too."

"Do you by any chance have that laptop with you?"

"Not on my person, no."

Matthews thought for a moment. "Would you be willing to provide your fingerprints and a blood sample? This would be voluntary. We can't compel you unless we charge you with a crime. So far all we have with you is an enigma with the mobile phone issue!"

"So why would you need them?"

"Process of elimination. If we find unidentified prints or bloodstains apparently connected to the murder then we can eliminate you without calling you back into the station."

"Okay then." Malcolm shrugged his shoulders. "Am I then free to go?"

"Yes, for the moment, but it is possible we may have some more questions for you. Will you still be staying at the Premier Inn? "

"No. I was hoping to drive home after this meeting."

"I'd appreciate it if you didn't leave Exeter before midday tomorrow, and check with us before you depart.

"Oh bloody hell!" Malcolm showed his frustration. "I've checked out of Countess Wear. What do you expect me to do?"

"Have you got a friend in the area you could stay with?"

"Possibly," Malcolm replied irritably. "Can I make a quick call?"

"Go ahead."

Malcolm extracted his mobile, scrolled through the saved numbers, and dialled. The call was answered immediately.

"Simon? It's Malcolm here. Something's cropped up, and they want me to stay in Exeter until tomorrow. Can I take you up on your offer of a bed?" He listened to the reply. "Thanks, very much, I'll be with you shortly. Oh, by the way, what's your address? You showed me roughly where it was yesterday."

Matthews handed Malcolm a pen and notepad for him to scribble down the address.

"Okay, this is where I'll be tonight. I hope I won't need

to stay longer."

After Malcolm had departed, Matthews ran his hand through his hair and said, "Do you think we are any further forward, Bob?"

"Not really. Weston seems pretty open and unworried by it all, unless he's a bloody good actor and he's certain that he's left no traces. I have the feeling however that he might know more about Patty than he is letting on. But two different women with possibly the same name and phone?"

"I think it would be worthwhile finding out a little more about our victim, Patty Gallagher."

Conveniently, Frank Gallagher was working at a house in Brookfields Road, almost in walking distance from the Police Station. Nevertheless, the officers drove there. They found him sitting in the driver's seat of his pickup, drinking coffee from a thermos.

"Sorry I can't offer you some," he said. "You've got some news?"

"We have identified the body, Mr Gallagher." Matthews paused. "I regret to say that it is Patty, your wife."

Frank shook his head then slumped forward, his free hand supporting his head. "It's all my fault," he murmured.

Matthews couldn't believe his ears, "Are you saying that you killed her?"

"No, no, no, I'd never do that. I loved her. I shouldn't have sworn at her that morning. She went off - and now she's … she's not coming back!" Frank Gallagher looked as if he were going break into tears.

"We have reports that you have been violent to your wife in the past, and you have already told us that it's not the first time she has gone off for a few days after an argument," said Sergeant Nicholls.

"Bloody nosy neighbours. Yes, I have slapped her occasionally when she had done something really stupid that made me angry. But never with the intention of harming her. I loved her."

"When you'd had too much to drink perhaps?" Nicholls

came back.

"I don't drink, not now. That's how I met her, at an Alcoholics Anonymous group. I was a heavy drinker back in my younger days, frequently stoned out of my mind. Until I had a health scare. But she had been in a far worse state than me, really fallen into the gutter, she had, with drinking and probably drugs too. Wasn't past using her body to earn some cash to pay for it, I believe." His voice breaking up, he paused.

Nicholls and Matthews looked at each other, anticipating that they were going to find valuable background on Patty Gallagher.

Gallagher blew his nose and continued. "But she was really a lovely woman. With the help of a friend she'd managed to pull herself together and, I suppose, start a new life. Apparently she was quite a bright girl, came from a good family, so she said. I never met her parents. She had been an undergraduate at Exeter, until she dropped out. Then her life went downhill fast."

"Did she say why she dropped out of university?"

"No, she wouldn't talk about it. I did try to get her to tell me but she just said, 'It's best you don't know'. So I don't."

"Do you know the name of her friend that helped her? Is the same one she stays with in Topsham?"

"Yes. Her friend - I think she was one of your lot."

"What do you mean?"

"She mentioned a police officer - a woman - who had encouraged her to join AA."

"You don't happen to know she was?"

"Sorry, no. Patty was already part of the group when I joined, so I can only go by what she told me."

"Tell me, is there anyone who might have wished her harm? Someone she might have upset? Perhaps told someone giving her unwanted attention to get lost?"

"No, nobody I can think of."

"And she seemed normal - no trouble or worries on her mind.?"

"No really. She tended to keep things very bottled up if she had any worries, though she had seemed a little bit more reserved over the past two or three months..." Frank paused.

"Go on."

"She had a phone call, and as she put the receiver down I heard her mutter, 'dead'." She looked a bit pale, and I asked her if everything was alright. She just said she was okay, so I didn't press her. I suspect something had triggered a memory from her past."

Nicholls started to say, "Do you own ..." but a hand sign from his boss stopped him.

"Thank you, Mr Gallagher, for your time. We will need to speak to you again, no doubt, but we'll let you get back to your work."

"Thank you. I'm not really feeling inclined to work at the moment but I suppose it will take my mind off things."

On their way back to the station, Bob Nicholls asked, "Why didn't you want me to ask Gallagher about the hammer, sir?"

"It would have been very stressful if he genuinely had nothing to do with his wife's death. I'd like to show him the hammer to see if he recognises it. Definitely need to speak to him again. Also, I'd like to have a word with Weston again before he buggers off to Brighton. He's all innocent and relaxed in his manner but I'm sure there's something he's not telling us."

*****

Malcolm followed Simon's car back to his house in Broadclyst, and parked in a nearby public car park next to the village hall. He had only just put his bags into a spare bedroom when he received another call from the police asking him back 'to clear up one or two further points'. "Look," he said, "I appreciate that you are investigating a murder but really I don't see what further help I can give you."

"I understand. I hope we won't keep you too long." said Inspector Matthews. "We have now spoken with Patty Gallagher's husband, and something cropped up that you might be able to clarify."

"Really?" Malcolm said with surprise. "All right, I'll be with you soon. "

Malcolm turned to his friend. "There's something else the police want to ask me about Patty Gallagher. God knows what."

"I don't like the sound of this at all, Malcolm." Simon thought for a moment. "Look, I think it would be a good idea if you take me through the whole scenario, of why you came to Exeter, and everything you have done since you arrived, in as much detail as possible. Leaving our even the smallest and seemingly insignificant detail could be crucial in defending any charge they might bring against you."

"Do you really think they could do that?"

"I've known charges to have been brought based purely on circumstantial evidence – and that's really all they have got at the moment." and silently to himself Simon added "I hope."

Again Malcolm recounted without interruption the full story, from the reason for his initial Flirty contact with Tricia to his first contact with the police. Simon scribbled down some notes.

"Okay, I can see why you are under suspicion but they need something else to bring you in."

Malcolm mentioned the Flirty message he had seen on his laptop. "I'm pretty certain the photo there was Patty. All of this Flirty stuff and the email are on my laptop. I did mention that to the police earlier, thinking that would verify my account. They asked if I had the laptop with me."

"And have you?"

"I told them I didn't have it with me, which was true. I didn't take it to the police station

"Oh hell," sighed Simon, "That's all they need! Where's your laptop now?"

"In my bag upstairs."

"Okay, I'm going to take it and deal with it. Do not under any circumstances tell the police about this message, and don't tell the police I've got the laptop unless I okay it with you."

"Do you think they are going to arrest me?"

"I hope not, but I couldn't guarantee. They may want to question you under caution. If so, say nothing until I arrive".

"Okay."

"Now, some questions about what you have told me. Firstly, the contact with Tricia on the website. Are you sure that you've never seen her before?"

"Never, though as I said, she did remind me of Barbara."

"Could she be related?" Simon looked at the photo Malcolm had provided. "Not all full face pic, is it. Almost as if she wasn't aware she was being photographed."

Malcolm shrugged his shoulders. "Never really thought about it. Unlikely but possible I suppose. Barbara did have a daughter from her previous marriage but I never met her. They didn't have any contact with each other."

"And what was it that led you to this Flirty website?"

"An email advertising, so it seemed, the opportunity for old people on their own, like me, to find companionship. Seems as if all four of us from college would qualify!"

"Charlie always has been a confirmed bachelor, and William is quite reticent about his life up the Midlands. I don't think he's been married. And I'm not looking to get married again. Once was enough."

"Something similar had been mentioned around a pint with friends."

"Could one of your drinking companions have sent the email?"

"Possibly, though I don't know why they would, except as a joke."

"Would any of them also have been in this 'old people on their own group'?"

"Well, Barney - he's the one looking after my cat - has a

ring on his finger but I've never seen any sign or mention of a wife. And one of the other chaps is widowed."

"Now let's look at the victim. Are you sure you don't know her?" Simon emphasised 'her'

"I don't know Patty Gallagher."

"That's not quite what I asked. Did you recognise the person in the photograph? Please be honest with me."

Malcolm paused before replying, "Not at first but she was vaguely familiar."

"And have you come to any conclusions about where you might have seen her?"

"A girl I knew at university as Patsy. But it's forty odd years ago and one might say that even the fairest flower wilts with time. You might have known her too."

"No, I didn't. I suggest you keep your answers rather simpler if - or shall I say, when – the police ask you that question again."

Malcolm nodded.

"How well did you know Patsy?"

"We went out together a few times."

"And, er, did you … ?"

"No, I didn't sleep with her, if that's what you are suggesting. I believe her parents were very religious, and very strict. No sex before marriage, that sort of thing. Though she was sexy, good looking and quite a charmer. "

"Why did you stop seeing her?"

Malcolm shrugged, "No particular reason. She just wasn't around any more. No shortage of other young fellows probably more appealing than me."

"If they ask I think you should mention this possible connection with Patty to the police. Better than them finding out themselves and accuse you of lying or withholding information. However, Malcolm, we'll leave it there for now.."

"Okay."

"Now you'd better make your way back to the police station – no, on second thoughts I'll drive you there. I need to make a phone call first, so how about you unpack your stuff and we'll set out in, say ten minutes?"

"Okay."

Although it had been at least half an hour since Malcolm had received the call from Matthews he was not expecting a police car to pull up outside Simon's house. Simon answered the door, with Malcolm standing behind him.

Detective Inspector Matthews addressed Malcolm directly, "Dr Malcolm Weston, we would like you to come with us to the police station for a formal interview under caution in connection with the murder ….."

The rest of the statement was drowned by Malcolm's cry, "What!" and Simon simultaneously saying, "That's ridiculous!"

Matthews completed the statement, " ... the murder of Patty Gallagher."

"Are you arresting me?"

"Not yet, unless you refuse to accompany us."

Simon regarded his friend with concern. "Malcolm, you are going to need legal advice. Are you happy for me to represent you?"

Malcolm had gone very pale "Yes, thank you. I don't know any other solicitors in Exeter." he murmured. "I don't understand. I haven't done anything!" He suddenly thought of something that required urgent attention. "Shylock my cat! Can you contact my friend and ask him to look after him – and just keep an eye on the house? I don't know at this rate when I'm going to get back home!

"Of course, let me have his name and phone. What do you want me to tell him? He'll be wondering why you don't contact him yourself."

"Say … er ..say I'm indisposed, been in an accident, taken ill … I don't know ! But don't say I've been arrested." The police were getting ready to lead him to the car. "Here's my keys – my car is in the car park across the road."

"I'll get on to him straight away." He then spoke to Matthews. "I will be with you at the station shortly. In the meantime I am advising Dr Weston not to answer any questions."

Chapter 8

"It's for you," Molly said, passing the phone over to her uncle. She had only just arrived back and had picked up the receiver from the small table by the front door.

Barney listened to the call, furrowing his brow. "Do you know what happened?" he asked the caller. "I see. Well, give him my best wishes, and not to worry. I'll look after Shylock."

"Shylock?" queried Molly.

"He's my neighbour's cat. He asked me to feed the moggie for the weekend while he was away. Seems he's been taken to hospital. Hopefully nothing serious." He looked at his watch. "Shylock will be wanting his supper, no doubt. He will have scoffed all the dried food I put down for him this morning."

"Can I come with you? I love cats."

"Of course."

Barney wasn't strictly her uncle. Molly was the daughter of his niece, Sally, who lived in London. It was an academic point, however, since 'uncle' fitted the bill for all concerned. In her first year at Sussex University, Molly has lived in a hall of residence and then shared a student flat in her second year. On a visit to Uncle Barney soon after he had moved the previous Easter from his former abode in Hangleton, Hove, to this new home just off Carden Avenue in Brighton, he had offered her a room, if she wanted accommodation for her final year. She had discussed this with her parents, and they had agreed that it was a win-win situation; Molly would have low-cost lodgings much closer to the university and Barney would have the benefit of some young blood from the family around the house.

"Who is your neighbour?" Molly asked as they walked the short distance uphill.

"Malcolm Weston. He's lived here for ages apparently. Lost his wife not so long back."

"Not Dr Weston?" Molly said with surprise.

"Yes, you know him?"

"He was one of my tutors in my first year. You know, I was sure it was him I saw when I visited you here back in the summer and I've seen him a couple of times since."

"What did you think of him?"

"He seemed very nice and mild mannered. I remember joking to Mum and Dad when we were talking about me staying here that I could always call and ask him for advice if I got stuck on a project. He didn't ogle the females students like a couple of the other lecturers. I always avoid wearing a low-cut blouse when I'm in their seminars. "

Barney chuckled. Molly was certainly well-proportioned in that area.

*****

Simon made a second call after he had finished with Malcolm's neighbour.

"Is Mr Coombes still in his office?"

"Yes, I think so. Who shall I say is calling?"

He gave the receptionist his name and waited.

"Simon! What a surprise! What can I do for you?"

"Glad you're working late, Charlie. I think the Express & Echo has already reported the discovery of a woman's body in the Exe."

"Yes, that's right."

"This is not for public release yet, but I wanted you to know that the police have taken in Malcolm for questioning for that woman's murder."

"You must be joking! Malcolm wouldn't harm a fly!"

"My thoughts exactly. I'm going to the police station shortly and will be representing him. I don't know what evidence they have against him but I can't believe that he would kill anybody, let alone a stranger."

"Well, if anyone can help him you can. He doesn't know the woman then? Does she have a name?"

"I'm pretty sure the police have identified her, so you'll

probably get a press release soon, with news of the arrest. Malcolm denies any knowledge."

"Right. Thanks for head up. Is there anything you want me to do?"

"If you can be fairly neutral about Malcolm in your reports that would be good, but unlike the Express and Mirror I know you don't go in for sensational and biased headlines. Also any probing into the background could be useful. I feel there's something odd about this but I can't put my finger on it."

Chapter 9

"Dr Weston, I'm going to summarise the caution I gave earlier, so there can be no misunderstanding.

"I'm not saying anything until Mr Cook gets here. I just don't understand … I …" Malcolm decided to stop there in case he did say anything that might be taken down and used against him.

"Very well, while we are waiting I'd like you to have another look at the photograph of Patty Gallagher that I showed you earlier." Matthews handed over the photo.

A tap on the door, and a uniformed sergeant put his head inside, "Excuse me, sir, but there's a Mr Cook waiting to see his client."

Matthews groaned inwardly. He knew Simon had a reputation for being tenacious like a dog with a bone, and not content until he'd chewed up evidence against a client and regurgitated it in his client's favour. When Simon was seated he began the interview.

"Now, Dr. Weston, earlier you told us that you did not recognise her. Would you care to have another look?"

Malcolm studied the photo for nearly half a minute, pursed lips, and said quietly, "No."

"We understand that she was at Exeter University probably around the same time that you were there. Are you sure you don't know her?"

"I've told you, I don't know Patty Gallagher!"

"She wouldn't have been Gallagher then. Any other Patty, or Tricia perhaps? Once again, I must ask you, do you recognise her?"

Malcolm looked at Simon, who gave a brief nod. "It is possible that she may be a girl, Patsy, whom I knew at university. The shape of her face seemed similar but if it is the same person she looks very different from forty odd years ago."

"Why didn't you tell us this earlier?"

"I wasn't sure. It was only when you told me the

49

woman's name that I began to wonder. I might have some ..."

"I think that's enough for now! Simon interrupted.

Matthews glared at Simon. "Dr Weston, I'll be frank with you. We have a dead body. We have you in the area at the time with no alibi. We have a phone with the victim's prints on it and suggestive messages to you. And we now have a possible link between you and the victim. Can you see why we have reason to suspect you?"

"I suppose so. But I didn't kill her. If it is the girl I knew at university I haven't seen her since."

"Now Dr. Weston," Matthews continued, "we must also advise you that we found a bloodstained hammer along the river bank, not far from where the body was discovered. Quite close to the Port Royal where you were supposedly waiting for your Tricia to turn up. The blood matches that of the victim, Patty Gallagher." .

"May we see the hammer?" Simon asked.

At his superior's request Nicholls left the room and returned shortly afterwards carrying a large plastic evidence bag containing a large claw hammer. Brown stains could be seen on its face.

"Recognise it?" asked Matthews.

Malcolm shook his head.

"For the record, please. Do you recognise the hammer?"

"No. It's not mine," Malcolm whispered.

"We have also found fingerprints on the handle," Matthews said.

"Were there more than one set of prints?" Simon interjected.

Matthews turned to his sergeant. "Bob?"

"Yes"

Malcolm looked puzzled. "What does that mean, Simon?"

"If there were only one set then they would have been from the last person to handle it without gloves. With other prints someone, or perhaps more than one person, would have used it either before or after. Am I right, inspector?"

Matthews nodded, thoughtfully. That possibility had probably not occurred to him.

"Have you matched those prints yet?" Simon asked. "I believe Dr Weston volunteered to provide his fingerprints."

"Yes he did. And, no, we are awaiting the results."

"In that case, until you do get a match, which I am sure will exonerate my client, you have no firm evidence against him." Simon rose, and said to Malcolm, "We're leaving."

"Just one moment, Mr Cook." Matthews said, his voice rising, "We know Dr Weston was in the area, and we have the evidence of the phone..."

"Which does not provide evidence of murder." Simon interrupted, "Now, are you going to charge him?"

Malcolm looked at Simon in consternation.

Matthews shook his head.

"Very well, we are leaving. Dr Weston will be staying at my house and will be available for further questioning if necessary."

"Thank you," said Malcolm to Simon as they left the building.

Neither spoke on the drive back until they were nearly back in Broadclyst. "One point I need you to think carefully about" said Simon, "In the unlikely event that they do find your prints on the hammer ..."

"I didn't kill her. I've never seen that hammer!"

"I believe you," said Simon, "but if you are innocent then we have to come up with a rational explanation of how your prints came to be on it. Ideally verifiable. I want you to think back very carefully for any occasion recently - or let's say, in the past few months - when you would have had an occasion to handle such an implement."

"I don't know. I've got a small hammer along with a few other common tools like a screwdriver and spanner but I'm not into D.I.Y."

"I'm not saying it was yours. Only a total idiot would commit a murder with their own weapon and then leave it to be found with their prints all over it."

"Thanks for your confidence in me."

Chapter 10

Simon found a message on his mobile. 'Call me back. Charlie." He took the opportunity of returning the call while Malcolm was still upstairs sorting out his things,

Charlie answered on the first ring. "Simon, what's the latest?" He listened to Simon's summary. "Okay, now I've got some information for you. As you expected the police released the name of the victim, and the usual bland statement that 'a man is helping with their enquiries, so they haven't named Malcolm yet" He paused for breath, "The name Patty Gallagher vaguely rang a bell, so I checked back in the archives to the year when she was likely to have got married, based on what her husband had told the press when we spoke to him. Her maiden name was Tanner. Do you recognise it? Patty - or Patsy - Tanner?"

Simon thought for a few moments before responding, "Yes, now you mention it, I do. Wasn't that the student who was raped at a student party? It was when we were also students."

"Correct."

"But what bearing would this have on Malcolm's present predicament?"

"I don't know, but the police are bound to find the same connection in due course. It might bring more suspicion on him."

"Malcolm has already told them he might have known her at university. I managed to stop him blurting out that he might have photos of her at home I don't want to give an excuse for the police to search his home but I fear that Malcolm may already have let the cat out of the bag in that respect."

"Very sad about Patsy, really," Charlie mused. "The rape ruined her life. She didn't become pregnant, thank goodness, but her parents threw her out of their home, claiming that she'd brought it all upon herself through flirting with boys. Ruddy sanctimonious religious nutcases - no concept of the meaning of the Christian message of love, forgiveness and compassion - they would have probably killed her themselves if she had been carrying a baby. Poor lass dropped out of university, and was virtually living on the streets."

"But wasn't her attacker identified?"

"Oh yes, another student. Sentenced to eight years but he probably served less than that."

"Right, well, thanks very much for the information. I'm not sure whether I can use it but it's always helpful to be one step ahead of the police. Oh, by the way, I wonder if you can help in another matter."

"Yes?"

"Malcolm claimed that he was going to meet a woman called Tricia, and had printed off a photo she sent. We have absolutely no idea who she is, or even if she exists, but her phone message to Malcolm was discovered on the mobile found near Patty's body. It would be very helpful to know who is in the photograph. Could you publish it with some blurb about wishing to identify the missing woman? I doubt if the police will bother. They think they've got the case wrapped up already."

"I'm sure we can do that. Send an image over on your phone if you can."

"Will do. We'll keep in touch. 'Bye."

The call reminded Simon that he urgently needed to have a look at Malcolm's laptop before the police got round to asking for it.

"Do you want me to show you what's there?" Malcolm asked.

"Probably quicker that way," said Simon.

The Flirty site showed confirmation of Malcolm's exchange of messages and photographs with 'OnlyOne' - the as yet unidentified Tricia. - which at least confirmed his friend's explanation for his visit to Exeter. Simon felt there was something he was missing from Malcolm's Flirty account. He spotted the recent, but unanswered message from a user named PayGal that Malcolm had mentioned earlier. Initial concern quickly escalated to serious alarm when he found the message had been sent at seven thirty on Saturday evening and the accompanying user photograph was undoubtedly that of Patty.

Simon realised that it would be a nail in the coffin for Malcolm if this information were to be discovered by Matthews. He couldn't also help wondering whether his client and friend was as innocent as he was claiming to be. Dodgy ground for him professionally, he thought, if he interfered with the data on Malcolm's laptop. He made coffee for them both while he considered possible options.

"We can't let the police see this," Simon said, "It will be one more important piece of circumstantial evidence that may tip the balance in whether or not to bring charges against you."

"You want me to delete it," Malcolm asked, his finger hovering over the keyboard.

"No, not yet," Simon said in haste, "We need to have a back up."

He made both a paper copy and a USB drive back-up of the messages from Malcolm's flirty page from Tricia and Patty.

Simon remembered Malcolm telling him that his attention had originally been drawn to Flirty by an unsolicited email. On the off-chance that it had not been deleted, Simon asked him to check his gmail account. Fortunately Malcolm had been very slack in clearing his email, with entries in his inbox alone going back some eighteen months, while some others had been stored in various folders. His bin was also quite full, although emails there were automatically deleted after a specific period of time.

He found the email, which looked quite innocuous, basically saying, '*There is no need to be alone. You can find someone who can share your life and interests*', with a link that connected to the Flirty site. There was no indication at all of who had sent the email.

"Malcolm, if it's okay with you, I'd like to get this email and your Flirty messages checked over to see if we can find who actually sent them. Can you let me have your passwords? You can always change them later."

Simon was a regular and experienced user of the internet but he didn't have the skills to trace the origin of emails or to hack into websites, but he knew someone who could. A former client, whom he'd successfully defended against a charge of scamming, now ran a small computer servicing business on the outskirts of Exeter. He checked his list of contacts and made the call.

"Miles Computing,"

Simon confirmed that he was speaking to the proprietor, Miles Hathaway, and explained what he wanted.

"I can do that. This is all above board, I trust?"

"Yes. I have a client who could be facing a serious charge, and I suspect that he may have been set up. It seems to have started through an email which directed him to a website. Ideally I'd like to know who sent the email and who contacted him through this website."

"Okay. Bring the laptop over to me. It may take a couple of days but it doesn't sound too big a challenge."

Chapter 11

Matthews was confident when he arrived at the station on Tuesday morning that the fingerprints on the hammer would enable him to close the case quickly. If he were a betting man he'd have put the odds at 60/40 in favour of Weston over Gallagher. He'd decided not to interview Gallagher again until he had the results.

His hopes were shattered by his sergeant. "You won't believe this, sir, one set of prints on the hammer belong to the victim."

"What? No way! You mean she smashed her own face in after she was dead then threw away the hammer?"

"I don't think so but it's certainly odd. They haven't got a match yet on the other prints but they are still working on trying to get an enhanced image on one smudged set."

"Bugger! We need to have another word with Gallagher!"

"What about Weston?"

"Hmm, he's still in my books for it. I'd rather he stays close at hand rather than shooting off back to Brighton."

"Have we got enough to hold him for further questioning?"

"If we can find another link to Patty then we could bring him in and probably keep him overnight, but Simon Cook won't give him up easily."

Fortunately they found Gallagher at home.

"You're lucky to catch me," he said, "I had to call back home to pick up some stuff for my next job, and I would not have been available for the rest of the day. I hope this won't take too long."

"We'll try not to keep you longer than necessary. We would like you to look at this," replied Matthews, passing over the hammer. "Is it yours?"

Gallagher took the plastic evidence bag, and examined it, turning it to get a closer look at the end of the handle, and frowned.

"Well?"

"I've got two or three such tools."

"It is yours, then?"

"It might be. I tend to scratch my initials on the end of the shaft . I started doing that when I used to work regularly with other blokes. But I don't think I got round to doing it with the last one I bought. I picked up a hammer and few other tools second-hand at a car boot sale. They hold them regularly down at Marsh Barton Trading Estate you know."

"When would this have been? Nicholls asked.

"A few weeks ago. Is this ... is this the weapon ... ?"

"Yes, it has Patty's blood on it. And her fingerprints."

"So are you saying she had this hammer with her when she was killed?"

"Probably." Although another possibility had occurred to Matthews. It could have been put in her hand by her attacker after she had been killed. "We will need to have the names of your mates that you were with on Saturday evening, just to confirm what you told us earlier about your whereabouts."

"Okay."

"Oh, just one more thing. Did Patty have a computer?"

"She had an old laptop. Used it mainly for emails, I think."

"May we borrow it? It is possible she may have known her attacker, and could have been in touch by email."

"No problem. I just want you to find out who did this to Patty."

Matthews thought for a moment then added, "I don't suppose you know her password by any chance?"

"Sorry. I'm not even sure she used one but she wasn't into complicated when it came to technology. It would have been something simple, like her maiden name."

"Which was?" Matthews realised he should have asked this question much earlier.

"Tanner, she was Patricia Tanner."

"Okay," said Mathews, "Thank you. I think that's all for now."

Nicholls knew better than to interrupt his boss when he

was deep in thought. Eventually, as they approached headquarters, Matthews broke his silence. "I want you to follow up Gallagher's alibi for Saturday evening."

"You still have him in the frame as a suspect?"

"Yes, though my gut feeling is that he's innocent. We need to find out more about Patricia Tanner as she was. That WPC who helped Patty rebuild her life, she may well have some useful background. See if you can find out her name and where she is now."

"Will do. Are you going to hand over the laptop to our computer geeks?"

"Probably need to, but I'm going to have a look myself first just in case we can save us some time."

While Nicholls set about the task of digging out information on their victim, Matthews powered up her laptop. It was unsurprisingly password protected but after a couple of permutations of her maiden name and Christian name it opened up with Pattanner. He had no idea what email address or provider she had used, but with the Google icon displayed he tried that first as her internet access. He clicked on the gmail option and was presented with an abundance of electronic correspondence - more than two thousand. Patty has obviously not been bothered about clearing out her inbox, Matthews scanned down the first page and found nothing to attract his attention. The rest he left for later examination. He searched for the Flirty website in the browser. Matthews had never, even in the course of his job, accessed such a site although he was aware of their existence. He could see why some men would get aroused by what appeared to be on offer. Inevitably there was a sign in option for users. He chanced the same password he had used to open the laptop, and was quite amazed when it worked.

There, displayed with her photograph, was Patty, under the user name PayGal. The screen displayed just one message she had sent: *Retribution for your sin.* Matthews frowned at the expression. It wasn't exactly inviting courtship or a sexual encounter. He looked at the date and recipient.

"Gotcha!" he exclaimed. The message had been sent to James111 at seven thirty on Saturday evening.

Chapter 12

Malcolm had been left on his own for most of the morning. Simon had needed to attend a meeting at his office after dropping off the laptop for examination by his computer technology contact. Malcolm was at a loose end; he could get the bus into Exeter and mooch around or just take a stroll around Broadclyst village. He opted for the latter, bought a newspaper and settled down with a coffee in Simon's conservatory, which was catching the morning sun. Although the police hadn't actually forbidden him from returning home, there seemed little point without his car, which was still being examined.

When he answered the doorbell and saw Inspector Matthews there, his rising hopes that he might finally be cleared from suspicion were quickly replaced by shock and fear at the detective's first words.

"Dr. Weston, we are arresting you on the suspicion on the murder of Patty Gallagher. You do not ...."

Malcolm scarcely heard the formal caution that followed as panic set in. Simon wasn't there to help him. He eventually found his voice, "I must leave a note for Simon," he croaked.

"Very well." Matthews accompanied him into the living room, where Malcolm scribbled a message on the notepad next to the telephone: 'I've been arrested. Help"

Matthews produced a pair of handcuffs and handed them over to a uniformed constable

"Do you really have to use them," Malcolm said, "I'm not going to do a runner or anything stupid."

The bobby looked at Matthews,who, after a short consideration. shook his head, and said, "Just bring him out to the car."

Simon's car screeched to a halt and as he climbed out he yelled, "What the hell's going on?"

Matthews closed his eyes in frustration, and replied as Simon stepped up to him, "We have arrested Dr Weston on the suspicion of the murder of Patty Gallagher."

Simon turned to Malcolm. "Say nothing! I'll be with you as soon as I can."

*****

Sergeant Nicholls had discovered a wealth of information about the earlier life of Patty Gallagher - or, rather, Patty Tanner as she had appeared in the police archives, which had taken him a couple of hours to sort through, let alone consider the implications for his investigation. He was on his third cup of black coffee when his boss returned.

"I've just brought Weston in, and he's in the cells waiting for his solicitor. Have you got anything for me?"

"Well, we have the latest information from the pathologist. Seems that Patty was killed by an overdose of heroin, probably injected shortly before she was beaten. She could have been rendered unconscious earlier."

"So possibly abducted and drugged elsewhere, brought to the river, killed, and beaten. That would explain why no-one heard any cries."

"Could be. But there is an interesting point about the beating."

"Yes?"

"The hammer we recovered may have been used to inflict some minor injuries, possible before she died, but the major damage was done afterwards with something heavier - possibly a large smooth stone.

"That's weird. Why two different weapons and kill her with drugs? Someone really must have wanted her dead - hammer, drugs, stoning & drowning!"

"Two persons involved?"

"Possibly." Matthews said thoughtfully. "So we're looking for a large stone - or perhaps something like a small sledgehammer?"

"Hammer would be preferable." Nicholls shuffled his notes, and continued, "I've found some very interesting background on our Patty, though I'm not sure whether it's relevant to the case. You might like to get a coffee, sir. This will take some time."

Matthews shunned the watery apology for coffee dispensed by the station's vending machine, and had brought in his own percolator, which he was happy for Nicholls to share when they were working together.

Nicholls appreciated this perk. "I'll start at the beginning. Patty was born Patricia Ruth Tanner in Exeter, 1955. It appears she had a very strict upbringing by her parents, Joseph and Mary Tanner, who were devout Christians. She was known by her friends as Patsy. She was a bright girl, who attended Bishop Blackall Grammar School, as it then was, and was accepted at Exeter University to study English. Although her parents insisted that she continued to live at home, it seems that she began to enjoy some of the freedom of student life. During the Spring of her first year, she went to a party at a student pad in Mount Pleasant Road where booze and drugs were apparently flowing freely. Anyhow, due to a combination probably of both, she crashed out on a bed. When she came to, she found a male student partly dressed by the bed. She was also in pain down below and screamed for help. Another student called the police. She claimed she had been raped. It was obvious from the blood that she had been a virgin. The student, who was actually a co-tenant of the property, was charged and convicted of rape. He always denied it, of course, but it was his bed, he was undoubtedly present, and there was one condom missing from the open pack by his desk. The used one wasn't found but he could have flushed it down the loo."

"Jesus Christ! What was the name of the student? He could be a suspect for Patty's murder."

"My thoughts too. His name was Richard Eastman. He was given eight years. Do you want me to follow that up and find where he is now?"

"Definitely. Meanwhile I'm still liking Weston for the murder, from something I found on Patty's laptop." Matthews thought for a moment before asking, "Is that all?"

"No, and here's the interesting part. The police obviously interviewed all those that had been at the party. Our Malcolm Weston was among them."

"So we've got another link to Weston. What if he was the one who actually raped her?"

"Well, I suppose it's possible."

"Anyone else we know who was at the party?"

"Of the two dozen students interviewed Charlie Coombes was the only other name I recognised

"The Editor of the Express and Echo?"

Nicholls nodded. "There was a lot about Patsy Tanner on file. She had form. She was arrested on several occasions for possession of illegal drugs, shoplifting, and prostitution. The latter probably to pay for her habit. Oh, and I forgot to mention, drugs were also found in Eastman's possession."

"So … was she already a druggie or was it as a result of her assault that she became addicted?"

"Probably after. Her parents gave her no support whatsoever and cast her out of their life. She didn't go back to college and ended up living rough."

"Frank Gallagher must have seemed like her knight in shining armour after all that she'd been through."

"You're probably right, sir. Although as Gallagher said, it was actually one our WPCs who helped her on the road to recovery, after Patsy had spent a night in the cells, stoned out of her mind. She apparently took pity on her, and when Patsy poured out her woes, she persuaded her to go Alcoholics Anonymous. As you know, it was there she met Gallagher."

"Is she still on the force? This WPC?"

"Her name was Billie Webster, but I haven't had time to track her down yet."

"Okay, you can leave that till later. I think it's more likely to be background than anything crucial to our investigation. In the meantime, we'll need to hear what Weston has to say about the party."

"Probably pissed as newt as well."

"And, while we're at it, we need to advise him of our intention to search his house. I think he was about to mention some old photos when his lawyer shut him up."

*****

When advised of the new findings that could be used against his client, Simon requested the opportunity to have a chat with Malcolm before he was questioned again by the police.

Malcolm was looking rather haggard but otherwise seemed to be bearing up well. Simon brought him up to date on the information he'd been given, including the last message supposedly from Patty. "Until I've had a report back about your laptop from my computer expert I think it would be best for you to deny that you even saw the PayGal message"

Malcolm looked at him and raised an eyebrow. Simon nodded. "Matthews hasn't asked you to produce your laptop yet, but he surely will. Don't let on that I've got it."

"This has got to be a set up, surely, though I cannot for the life of me think why."

"You're probably right, Malcolm, but until we have proof, or can come up with a credible explanation of why someone else must have done it, I'm afraid that police have the upper hand at the moment." Simon paused, then added, "I'm not sure what line of questioning Matthews is going to take this afternoon but please just let me give you a nod before you reply. Sometimes seemingly innocuous questions have some hidden barbs, and I don't want you to get caught out."

The questions from Matthews were first of all concerned with events in the distant past. "Now, Dr Weston, we know you were at a student party in 1974 at which Patty - or Patsy, as she was then known - was raped. You knew that? "

'Yes," replied Malcolm quietly.

"Why didn't you tell us?"

"You didn't ask."

"Did you rape Patsy at that party?"

Simon spoke sharply, "I must protest. You have no basis whatsoever for that accusation. You know very well that another student was convicted."

"Ah, yes, Richard Eastman. How well did you know him?

Malcolm glanced at Simon before replying. "Not all that well. We were both studying English, so we obviously knew each other in that respect but he had his own group of friends."

"Yet you went to his party?"

"He invited everyone on that same course. Most of them came."

"What did you think of him as a person? Did you get on well together?"

"I didn't like him much. He was a rather arrogant young man, full of his own self-importance. Fancied himself – and anybody wearing a skirt and well stacked."

"Bit of a Romeo then?"

"You could say that. He had that reputation."

"So you weren't surprised when he was charged with rape?"

"Actually I was a bit. He could have had his pick of girls willing to sleep with him without forcing himself upon them. Though Patsy wouldn't have let him."

"Perhaps that was a blow to his ego if she turned him down."

"Possibly."

"Right, let's come back to Patsy. What do recall of her at that time?

"As I've said before, she came from a strict religious background. Quite reserved and shy at first but she really came out of her shell in the company of other students, She knew how to use her natural good looks to flirt with the lads but she would never let anyone an inch above her knee, so to speak. Very reluctant to talk about anything of a sexual nature"

"Yet she was your girlfriend?"

"Again, as I've already told you, we went out a few times. Strictly platonic relationship, for the reasons I've mentioned."

"Did you go to the party with her?"

"We arranged to meet there. When I arrived she was already enjoying herself, and attracting the attention of Richard and his other flatmates, like bees aound a honeypot they were. I didn't really get much chance to talk to her that evening."

"It didn't bother you that she'd ditched you in favour of others?

"Hardly ditched. I wasn't really bothered. I'd just said, 'like to come to a party?' and she said, 'see you there'. She might have already had an invite."

"What can you remember about the events of that night?"

"In detail, not much. I got to the palace, as they called it ..."

"Why palace?" Nicholls interjected.

"Someone had once joked that all four tenants were named after kings – Richard, Charles, William, and Stephen."

"You wouldn't have fitted in then," sneered Nicholls.

"Only if I'd used my middle name. But I had no desire to share a flat with Richard."

"You were telling us about the party," said Matthews, giving his sergeant a disapproving look for interrupting the flow of Malcolm's narrative.

"I got there about 8 pm, and the party was already well under way. I chatted to various people I know, chatted up one or two other girls as well, I think, but I had quite a bit to drink. I've never been a heavy drinker, and I suspect as the evening wore on I'd probably have been propping up the door post with a smile on my face."

"Do you remember who else was there?"

"Well, apart from those I've already mentioned, no, not really. There must have been a couple of dozen."

"Did you see Patsy go upstairs?"

"No, I don't think so."

"Did you go upstairs at any time?"

"Er, I'm not sure. I might have gone to the loo just before I left. The downstairs one was, um, not a nice place to be."

"Was the party still going when you left?"

"Yes, though I guess things were beginning to wind down."

"What time would this have been? "

"God, I don't know. Perhaps ten thirty, eleven o'clock?"

"Did anyone see you go, or did you say goodbye to anyone, anyone else leave with you?"

"I waved goodbye to Richard but I'm not sure whether he noticed me or not."

"Where were you living at the time?"

"Not far away, Portland Street."

"Was anyone else at home when you arrived back there?"

Malcolm looked at Simon, "You were in, I think."

Matthews looked at Simon. "You were at university together?"

Simon nodded, "Yes I was. And before you ask, I hadn't been to the party. I was in when Malcolm returned but I can't be sure of the exact time."

"I see." Matthews obviously wasn't happy. "But, Dr Weston, you definitely were not at the Mount Pleasant address when the police arrived?"

"No. But they did interview me next day. If you look back at the reports you'll probably find a better recollection of events from me than over forty years later!"

"We will do that," said Matthews. "Now, coming back the events of the last few days, we have found an interesting message on Patty's laptop."

Simon looked at Malcolm who just shrugged his shoulders, appearing puzzled. Good acting, Simon thought.

"It seems that Patty had registered under the name PayGal on the Flirty site, and her photograph was on view.

She sent a message to a James111 – you are registered there as James111, am I correct?"

Malcolm looked at Simon and nodded

"For the record, please."

"Yes, James111 is my user name on the Flirty site."

"Now this message was sent to you at seven thirty on Saturday evening. That would not be long before she was killed. Can you explain that?"

"I don't know about that message. I haven't seen it."

"Are you sure?"

"Yes, for two reasons." Malcolm had the response which he had discussed with Simon prior to the interview. "Firstly, as you commented on when you first interviewed me at Countess Wear, I got myself pretty drunk in my room that Saturday evening and surfing the internet wasn't in my plans. Secondly, the name PayGal would have not meant anything to me and it wasn't until much later that you showed me a photograph of Patty, which I didn't recognise at the time."

"Very well." Matthews was not convinced that Malcolm hadn't seen the message, but could not fault his logic. One thing puzzled him, however. "How would Patty have known your Flirty user name?"

Malcolm thought deeply before replying. "I've been wondering about that, too. It's very likely that she knew my middle name is James. It is possible that if we were talking about the palace – Richard's pad – at some time I could have mentioned that I'd would be James 111, given that I was the third generation of Westons with that Christian name. But even so she would have had to make an inspired guess."

Matthews had come across even more unlikely explanations that turned out to be correct. "I think we're just about finished. We would however like to search your home, particularly for anything relating to Patty or Patsy. We don't actually need your permission as we have a warrant, but if you could provide us with a front door key if would save any damage from a forced entry."

Malcolm once again looked at Simon, who nodded. "Okay. There is a spare key under the geranium pot by the back door. I've got nothing to hide but please leave the place tidy if you can. And look out for Shylock, my cat. He's being looked after by a neighbour."

Simon added, "I would like to be present during the search. I'm sure you don't want there to be any accusations of planting evidence, though I have no reason to believe that you would do so."

Matthews grimaced but conceded. "You observe, that's all. You do not obstruct. Is that clear?"

"Yes, agreed. Now what about Dr Weston?" Simon said.

"I'm afraid Dr Weston will be detained here overnight. Normally we can hold you only for twenty four hours without charging you but I am going to request an extension to allow us time to search your home tomorrow. "

"Could I come with you to the house? I need to pick up some clean clothes anyway," Malcolm asked.

"'May I have a quick word with my client?" Simon interjected before Matthews could reply.

While the inspector and sergeant withdrew, Simon tried to calm Malcolm's obvious distress at the thought of being locked up for two nights at least. "Malcolm, I would usually object to such a request, but I think it does make sense in the circumstances. I'm not happy that you would be on your own in the car with Matthews for several hours, and I can't see him agreeing to you travelling with me. Nothing is going to happen until Matthews has seen your house, and I need some extra time to see what my computer geek comes up with. We are fortunate that Matthews still hasn't formally asked you to hand over your laptop. I suspect he's expecting to find it at your house."

"I see your point. So how long can they hold me?"

"For a serious crime such as murder they can apply for an extension of up to four days."

"You're joking!"

"'Fraid not. At the moment, on balance, I think they have enough circumstantial evidence to persuade a magistrate to grant that extension but certainly not enough to convince a jury of your guilt beyond reasonable doubt."

"I'm feeling seriously pissed off about this whole affair!"

"Understandably. But on the plus side, you haven't been sent on remand to Exeter Jail, and even if you were released I'm pretty sure they would want you to stay in the area. I'm confident that I'll be able to sort things out in your favour."

Simon put the suggestion that Malcolm could accompany him to Brighton, but as he anticipated his request was refused.

After Malcolm had been led away, Simon gathered up his papers and spoke to the Inspector, "I will see you tomorrow in Brighton at Dr Weston's house. Shall we say midday?" He paused, then added, "Off the record, how do you feel about this case?"

"We've had convictions previously with less evidence than this," Matthews replied. "We've got time, place, and weapon and even a motive."

"And you're happy with that?"

"Well, wouldn't you be? There are a couple of unanswered questions but I'm sure they will get resolved."

Simon shook hands with the detectives and took his leave.

Nicholls said to his boss, "You sounded a little uncertain in your reply to Weston's solicitor, sir."

"Did I? Seems pretty well cut and dried to me … although there are indeed some points on which I'd like further information, as they could have a bearing on the case."

"Such as?"

"We still do not know whether this Tricia, whom Weston claims he was going to meet, is a real person or whether it's just some random photo he's using to divert our attention. I think he also knew Patty rather better than he's letting on."

"What about the hammer?"

"Yes, that too. Shame about the unidentified prints. It

does seem a little odd that while he's obviously taken great care to dispose of anything that could have been used to identify the victim he was careless enough to leave her mobile nearby to be discovered, and also not to have made sure that the hammer would not be found."

"Perhaps he thought he had chucked it in the river."

"Wouldn't you have made certain, in his position?"

"Yes, I would. Although it would have been dark."

Chapter 13

"There's a police car just pulled up outside Dr Weston's house," said Molly.

"Really?" replied Barney in surprise.

"And there's now another car - no, two cars! "What's happening, do you think?"

"I don't know. I'll go and tell them that he's away for a few days."

Barney grabbed his coat and hat and headed up the pavement to Malcolm's place, where a uniformed constable stood just inside the gate. Barney saw a couple of men returning from the rear of the property, and another older man waiting with his hands in his pockets by one of the cars.

"What's going on?" Barney asked the constable, "Dr Weston's not home."

Nicholls was just about to try the key Matthews had handed to him in the front door lock. They turned at the sound of Barney's voice."

"Who are you sir?" Matthews asked.

"I'm Barney Newton. I live just down the road. I'm looking after Dr Weston's cat while he's in hospital."

"Who told you he's in hospital?"

Simon, who had heard the exchange as he stood by his car, said "I did." He turned to Barney and introduced himself. "I'm Simon Cook, I'm Malcolm's solicitor. I'm the person who phoned you the other day. I didn't want to worry you unduly at the time, but I regret to say that he has been charged with a very serious crime. These officers are from Exeter and have a warrant to search his house."

"Malcolm? I can't believe it! What's he supposed to have done?"

"He's been charged with the murder of a woman."

"Good Lord!"

"Look, can we have a chat when I've finished here? You may be able to tell me something about Malcolm that could help." Simon had noticed that Matthews and Nicholls had just entered the house.

"Of course. I'm just down there," he pointed, "the house with the new gates."

"Okay, see you later."

The policeman on watch at the gate had already been briefed about Simon, and let him through. In the hallway he stood and looked around. He poked his head into the front room where Nicholls was meticulously going through the contents of an old mahogany bureau. Simon could hear the sound of drawers and cupboards being opened and closed in another room. Well maintained and tidy house, Simon thought, for a widower living on his own.

He noticed a small pile of unopened letters behind the open front door. He gathered them up and put them in his jacket pocket, intending to tell Matthews when the search was completed.

A few minutes later, both officers had finished on the ground floor, and headed upstairs. Simon followed. Of the three rooms, one was obviously Malcolm's bedroom, one, with a rather musty smell, was probably rarely used as a guest bedroom, and the third had been converted into an office-cum-workroom. A rather old PC sat on the desk. Nicholls powered it up. "Needs a password," he called to his boss.

"Try Shylock," Matthews suggested.

It worked. Nicholls scanned the various files but failed to find anything of interest.

"We'll need to take this for further examination," Matthews said to Simon. And then, puzzled, said to his sergeant, "No sign of a laptop, Bob? I'm sure Weston mentioned one."

"It's in my possession," said Simon. "Malcolm left it at my house."

"Then why the hell didn't you say so! Might've saved us all this trip!" Matthews snarled.

"You didn't ask me, and, as I recall, you didn't even ask

Malcolm where it was."

Matthews just about held his temper in check but he was clearly annoyed and frustrated. "I want it as soon as we get back to Devon!"

They continued their search. On top of a wardrobe they found an old leather suitcase containing some old photo albums. Most were of no interest, consisting of black and white holiday family snaps. However, there were a few featuring Malcolm as a young man in the company of some other males and females of similar age. Matthews recognised the background in a couple of shots. "These were taken at Exeter University," he exclaimed. "And, look, that's surely Patsy!"

"May I see?" Simon asked.

Matthews handed the small bundle over to him.

"That's Charlie Coombes with William Forth and Patsy, I think. And Richard Eastman. I don't know the other girl." He looked at another photo. "And that's Malcolm with Charlie and me."

"I recall you mentioning that you were at university together," Matthews said. .

"Yes, and I'll also remind you that I wasn't at the party and I didn't know Patsy then."

"Have you kept in touch with Richard Eastman by any chance? You know he spent time in prison for raping Patsy."

"I've no idea what happened to him after he was released."

"Okay, I think that more or less concludes our business here. Er, what would you like me to do with the key? I don't think it's a good idea to leave it in a place that any burglar would be bound to search if he knew the house was unoccupied."

"I'll take it," said Simon. "Might be best if I let his neighbour hold it, if he's going to be looking after the cat, at least until any alternative arrangements are made."

"Fine. And don't forget about the laptop!"

"I'll bring it in tomorrow when I return to Exeter," And

after I've collected it from my hacker, Simon thought.

After Nicholls had carried out the computer and Matthews had left with the small bundle of photographs, Simon checked the house through to make sure there were no open windows and then locked up. Matthews had also searched the garage and the garden shed, but before leaving, and more out of curiosity than expectation of finding anything relevant, Simon wandered round to the well-tended back garden.

A couple of minutes later he knocked on Barney's front door.

"Hi there, are you okay for a chat?"

"No problem. Come in!" Barney invited him.

"Nice new fence you've got there I see," Simon commented.

"Yes, in fact Malcolm helped me put it up. He'd a good guy."

"Oh really?" A worrying thought entered his head. "Tell me, what did he actually do?"

Barney seemed surprised at the question. "Well, he did most of the heavy work, like securing the posts."

"For which he used a hammer or mallet?"

"Yes, of course. A hammer. Why?"

Shit, thought Simon. "Can I see it? I presume you've still got it."

"Hold on, I'll be right back," Barney turned towards the door, and then stopped, "Oh sorry, I should have introduced you. This is my niece's daughter, Molly."

"Hi Molly,"

"You're here about Dr Weston, aren't you?

"Yes. You knew him?"

"He was my tutor in my first year. Didn't think I'd end up living nearby. Of course, that's only in term time."

"Where's your home then?"

"I'm in London. Quite handy really, if I want to pop back on the train. Mind you, with all my books and stuff I need a car at the start and end of term."

"Do you drive?"

"I've passed my test but can't afford my own car. Either my dad or my uncle Sean drive me down."

Barney returned looking worried. "I can't find it anywhere! I'm sure it was there when I last looked."

"And when was that?" Simon was getting a distinct feeling of unease.

"Er, well, soon after the fence was finished, I suppose. You arrived later that same day, Molly."

"Is there anyone who could have borrowed it? Anyone who would have access to, to your garage I suppose? Any incidents of thefts of garden tools around here recently."

"I've not lent it to anyone, the garage is not locked during the day, and yes there have been the odd burglaries but I've not noticed anything else missing."

"Might just be worth checking." Simon realised that if Matthews were to get hold of this information it would make a strong but largely circumstantial case against Malcolm into something virtually indefensible. "I would appreciate it if you didn't report this to the police."

"Why not?"

Simon took a deep breath. "A hammer is believed to have been used in the assault on the dead woman. I really don't want the police seeing this as a link to Malcolm."

"You believe he really is innocent?"

"Yes I do, but believing is not the same as proving."

Simon accepted a cup of tea and biscuits, and chatted generally about Barney and Molly's impressions of Malcolm. He noticed that the saucer was of the same variety he had seen by Malcolm's back door. After he said goodbye to Barney and Molly, he returned to Malcolm's house. He carefully picked up the empty saucer with the few crumbs of dried cat food from beside Malcolm's back door and put it into a plastic bag. He'd let Barney have it back in due course.

Chapter 14

Simon made good time on his journey. The sections of single carriage highway across parts of Dorset and East Devon were remarkably free of heavy lorries, tractors and dawdling senior citizens that could reduce average speed considerably. He decided to take a short diversion and collect Malcolm's laptop rather than leave it until the following morning. It would also give him a little more time to act on anything that had been discovered before he handed the appliance over to the police.

He pulled over just after leaving the A30 dual carriageway at the Daisymount junction and made a call, As he had expected Miles Hathaway was at home, which was where he worked anyway. A short drive brought him to the premises in the village of Whimple, from where it was only three or four miles along minor roads to his own house in Broadclyst.

"Any joy," he asked.

"Well, some, though I'm not sure how helpful it will be. The email promoting the dating site was probably sent from this country but I'd need to probe further to find its origin. It certainly didn't come from Flirty headquarters in the Netherlands. I'm pretty sure, too, that the OnlyOne and the PayGal account were both set up by the same person. I haven't been able to link it to that email address, though if you gave me more time I might be able to get further."

"That's not really going to be possible. The police want this laptop tomorrow. I've been fortunate so far that they hadn't twigged that I might have it."

"Okay. One other thing, the photos of OnlyOne. I think the face and body are not of the same person."

"Really?"

"Here, take a look. First the mugshot of OnlyOne. Look closely at her skin where it's not covered by her blouse, to the left of her throat, then look at the same position where only a naked body below her chin is exposed. See the difference?"

Simon looked closely but couldn't make any distinction at first. The he noticed a small dark mole on the facial photograph in the position indicated. There was no corresponding mole on the body. "Got it!"

"It suggests to me that whoever posted these of Flirty, it wasn't OnlyOne - or Tricia, I think you said was her name. Whoever it was managed to get a photo of the girl, probably without her knowledge, but had no way of getting her to do a striptease for the sexy pose. It could be any clip he'd borrowed from a porn site or whatever. It wouldn't be difficult."

Simon offered his thanks to Miles together with twenty quid and took his leave. He was certain now that his friend had been set up but still had no idea why Patty had apparently enticed him through the Flirty site. He didn't have any evidence yet from Malcolm's laptop that would help acquit him of the murder charge. When he'd first seen the PayGal posting he had thought of removing it but now the police knew where it had come from they would obviously expect to find it on Malcolm's machine.

The information Miles had given him about the doctored photograph of Tricia triggered some thoughts, albeit ones that didn't make much sense, about who the mystery Tricia might be.

Later, after he'd had some supper, Simon rang Charlie, whom he expected now to be at home.

"Hi Charlie. I've just got back from Brighton. Kept an eye on things while the police searched Malcolm's house."

"Did they find anything useful?"

"I don't think so. A few old photos but nothing incriminating. You were in one of them with William, Patsy, Richard Eastman and another girl. Don't suppose you remember when that was taken?"

"Goodness knows. You know that I shared the house with Richard, William and another student that year? Before I moved in with you and Malcolm?"

"Er, yes, I remember."

"I would have moved out sooner. I didn't really like Richard very much."

"Why was that?"

"I didn't like his attitude to women. Always seemed to be shagging a different girl each week and boasting about it. Place was like his own personal brothel. Mind you, William also had a bit of a reputation that way as well!"

Since William had subsequently taken holy orders he must have seen the light at some point, Simon thought. "Were you the one who called the police?"

"No, that was Stephen, the other flatmate. I wasn't really into the party scene. I went for a walk to clear my head, and the police were there when I got back. Wasn't surprised at the outcome. Patsy was good company but, shall we say, sexually reserved - reserved for marriage probably. I doubt if Richard would have been happy if she rejected his advances. He thought he was god's gift to women."

"Are you still in touch with Stephen?"

"No. He was killed in a car crash only a few years after he graduated."

"Oh, one other thing. In fact the main reason for calling. Have you had any response to the publishing of Tricia's photograph?"

"Not yet. It's only been a couple of days."

"Okay. Well, let me know."

Simon remembered that he'd not yet examined Malcolm's mail. Two obvious mail shots he chucked in the waste paper basket. Three more were official communications from bank, credit cards services and the council. One was in a pale mauve envelope hand-addressed to Mrs B. Weston.

Chapter 15

"Weston's lawyer is asking again about the prints on the hammer, sir." Nicholls covered the phone mouthpiece with his hand.

Matthews groaned. "What does he want to know?" To strengthen their case against Malcolm they had put out an appeal for witnesses who may have seen him anywhere in the area of the crime scene on the Saturday evening. So far with no success.

"He wants to know whether we have yet identified the other prints."

"Let me talk to him."

Nicholls passed the handset over.

"Matthews here. There were two unidentified fingerprints on the handle and another less clear set. Why are you asking?" He listened to the reply and responded, "If you can tell me where these other prints came from I can see if there is a match." And after a further pause, "No, I am not going release the hammer for you to make independent tests! And I am still waiting for the laptop!"

At the other end of the phone, Simon shrugged, and ended the call. It had been worth a try. He couldn't risk the chance of the police finding a match between those on the hammer and those on Shylock's saucer. The inevitable conclusion they would draw is that Malcolm clearly had access to the murder weapon. Nevertheless, if Barney's hammer had been used on Patty, the presence of prints from both Barney, Malcolm and a third party could be very useful - if only Simon had someone in his sights that could have been responsible for the murder. It obviously could not have been Barney. However … he could get any prints lifted from the saucer and use these in evidence at a later date if relevant.

Matthews spoke to his sergeant again. "Make my day, Bob. Tell me you've had some joy in tracing Richard Eastman, so that we can eliminate him from our list of other possible suspects."

"You can definitely remove him, boss. He died back in the early summer this year. Seems he topped himself. "

"Any particular reason? Were you able to find out anything more about his background?"

"Apparently he'd had problems with depression over the years ever since he was released after serving about five years. Never went back to college to finish his degree. He moved back to London and drifted around from one menial job to another. Bright spot was that he married a young probation officer after a whirlwind courtship within a year of getting his freedom. They had a couple of kids."

"We've also had a chat to the bar staff at The Prospect," Nicholls continued, "Weston was definitely there on the Saturday lunchtime as he claimed, and he did show the photo of Tricia to them. I showed them photos of both Patty and Tricia but they couldn't identify either woman. However, they confirmed that Weston was there on Friday evening as well. The staff at the Port Royal think that Weston was there on Saturday evening but they were busy and couldn't be certain. He also told us that he'd called in at the Double Locks pub on Friday afternoon. I checked there and got a possible I.D."

"Did you show the photograph of Tricia and Patty to the Double Locks or Port Royal staff?"

"No I didn't. Do you think it's necessary?"

"Well, I'm doubtful about Tricia, but it is possible that Patty could have been there before she was killed.

"So nothing to give him an alibi."

"By the way, did you notice, sir, that Tricia's photo was in the Express & Echo, under a "missing person' blurb?

"Yes. Well, if she turns up it could be very interesting." Matthews thought for a few moments. "Where are we with the examination of Weston's car? Some fibres or hairs we could link to Patty would be good."

"It was collected from the car park in Broadclyst two days ago. I'll chase up forensics."

Chapter 16

Matthews was feeling under pressure. Though he could still hold on to Weston for another couple of days, time was short to delve into the data on his laptop that his lawyer had just brought in, and he was still awaiting results on Patty's machine. Simon Cook was currently talking to Weston in the cells and would no doubt be demanding action. Perversely, the hammer had yielded no sign of Weston's prints.

"How are you bearing up? Simon asked Malcolm

"I've felt better but I don't have to worry about getting my own meals. So what's the latest?"

"Well, I haven't found anything yet that's definitely puts you in the clear but I'm following up a lead with suggests that you have been set up, though goodness knows why. The police found nothing of interest at your house, and are currently examining your PC and your laptop."

Simon saw Malcolm's flash of concern. "Don't worry, there's nothing they can use against you on the Flirty site that they don't already know about. It's looking more and more likely that Patty was wanting to meet up with you for some reason - which of course might give you a motive." One question, though - when you helped your neighbour put up his fence, did you use a hammer?"

More alarm from Malcolm. "Oh bloody hell, yes! I'd forgotten. I suppose the police know about that!" He held his head in his hands. "Doesn't look good, does it?"

"No worries. The police don't know about it. I was talking to Barney after they had left. But the hammer has gone missing, and if you didn't take it, someone did! Of course, I don't know whether it is the same hammer as the murder weapon. I'd like to know whether any of the unidentified prints belong to Barney but I'm not sure how to do that without getting Matthews excited. Anyhow, leave that with me."

Simon opened his briefcase, withdrew the letters and

handed them over. "I picked these up from your house. If this drags on you may need to give me power of attorney to deal with any financial issues. And there's the letter addressed to your late wife."

Intrigued, Malcolm opened his wife's mail first and extracted two printed sheets. He looked at the address and then at the signature at the bottom of the second sheet.

"It's from Barbara's daughter!" he exclaimed.

"I thought you said they had not been in contact for over twenty five years?"

"That's right, though in her last couple of weeks, when she realised the end was nigh, she told me she wanted to write to her - and try to heal the rift. But of course, she had no idea where Sarah, her daughter, was. I suggested she should ask the solicitor that handled her divorce to pass the letter on to her ex-husband's solicitor, who might still have a contact for him, and thus to Sarah."

"It seems to have worked."

After Malcolm had read it through he handed it over to Simon. "Here, see for yourself."

Dear Mother,

By the time this letter gets to you I fear that you may already be at peace. It was only some time after returning from a family holiday that my father passed on to me your letter which had been forwarded by his solicitor.

I appreciate your frankness in trying to make amends for the real hurt that you caused me and which has kept us apart for so many years. I loved my father as a child - and we're still very close even though I'm married with children of my own. I loved you and thought that you loved me too. I was only 10 years old when you threw dad out of the house and took up with that fancy man. You didn't believe me when I told you that he fondled me in places that were embarrassing for a young girl and I was so glad to leave that house and live with Dad. I gather that you were dumped soon after he'd fleeced you of the money

Gran had left you. Serves you right, I'd thought.

I accept your apology without question. I only wish you had done so earlier. Though your treatment of dad - and me too, I suppose - still made me angry, part of me wanted to know what my mother was really like. But I could never bring myself to make than first contact.

It sounds as if you eventually found true happiness with another man if you have been with Malcolm for twenty five years. I would like to meet him some time. I understand that you never had more children, and he might appreciate being a step-grandad! I have never poisoned my children's minds about the failings of their grandmother. As far as they are concerned, you had just 'gone away'. Sadly that is now probably true.

Yours with love,
Sarah.

Malcolm wiped tears from his eyes."Not going to be great for her kids when she learns she's got them a jailbird for their grandad!"

"It may not come to that. Don't give up hope."

"All right for you to say that. You're not stuck here in a cell!" Malcolm took a deep breath and said more calmly, "I'm sorry, you don't deserve that. I know you're doing your best."

"I need to make contact with Sarah, if that's okay with you, and the sooner the better. Thankfully she's included a phone number, I suggest you write a note, keep your present predicament out of the picture as such, and say that circumstances won't allow you to meet just yet. Introduce me as your friend - I'll ring her to arrange a meeting, and take your letter with me. Easier for the explanation to come from a third party rather than you."

"Good thinking, Simon. Look, how about I sketch something out now on your notepad? I suspect that any letter I write from here would be scrutinised for any hidden messages, and I certainly don't want her troubled by the police for any reason."

"That would work" Simon removed the top sheet on which he had scribbled some notes and handed over the pen and pad."

"By the way, is Shylock okay?"

"I expect he misses you but he's being looked after well by your neighbour, Barney. I expect he's also getting some cuddles from his niece. She's in the final year at uni, and is lodging with him. You may remember her. Apparently you taught her in her first year."

"What's her name?"

"Molly. Don't know her surname."

"Pritchard. It would be Molly Pritchard. Lovely lass."

"Yes she was complimentary about you too."

"Come to think of it, I'm sure I saw her getting out of a car and unloading cases and books and what have you and an older chap helping. I presume it was her father who'd driven her down from wherever. I was going to offer to help Barney give the new fence a coat of preservative, but thought it best to leave it if he'd got visitors"

"I think she said it was her Uncle Sean."

Chapter 17

Dear Sarah,

I am so glad that you received your mother's letter. It was in truth her last wish that she wanted to make peace with you before she died. Sadly, she passed away in November last year, shortly after she had written it. I'm only sorry that you were not able to know her as the loving and caring woman with whom I enjoyed twenty five glorious years together.

I would love to meet you and your children in due course, but at present I am indisposed and not able to travel. I will not trouble you with the details in this letter. I have, however, asked my friend, Simon Cook, to get in touch with you on my behalf, and he will be able to explain the current situation in which I find myself.

My very best wishes,
Malcolm Weston.

Simon had thought about adding some more details to Malcolm's script but had decided, in keeping with his own advice, to leave it short and to the point. He sealed the envelope and addressed it to Mrs. Sarah Manning, using the name and address in Carshalton on her original letterhead.

The voice that answered sounded like a pubescent young teenager whose voice was about to break. "It's for you, Mum."

"Hello?"

"Sarah Manning? "

"Speaking."

"My name is Simon Cook. I'm a friend of Malcolm Weston. He has only just seen your letter to your mother who sadly passed away several months ago. He asked me to contact you."

"Yes I did wonder if I might be too late. Er, why is he not ringing himself. Is he ill?"

"No, he's in good health, but he's not at home at the moment. He's in Exeter."

"Okay ... so why is he not able to travel?"

"It's a long and complicated story but he is suspected by the police of committing a serious offence, and they are not allowing him to leave the city. I'm also his solicitor as well as his friend. I have very good reason to believe that for some reason that I do not yet understand, he is being set up to take the rap for this crime."

"I find it difficult to believe what you are telling me."

"Yes I realise that this would come as a shock. I would like to meet you in person to explain the situation fully ..."

"I'm not sure that I want to know!"

"Please, Mrs Manning. It is urgent. It seems that his predicament has been brought about as the result of something that happened a long time ago, before he even met your mother. But more crucially, it is possible that without your knowledge you have been used to lure Malcolm into a trap. I can only be certain if I can see you face to face."

"Well, I ... I don't know what to say. I've never met him and he's never met me."

"That actually is the basis for the deception, I believe. Please, for the sake of your mother, who would turn in her grave if she could see what has happened.."

"Very well. I work most days but I shall be at home tomorrow. Do you want to meet me there or somewhere else?"

"That's up to you. Somewhere where we have a little privacy to talk."

"Are you also coming from Exeter? Driving?"

"No, I shall take the train to Waterloo."

"All right, so your best bet is to change at Clapham Junction and get a local train to Carshalton. I suggest we meet at the Sun Inn, which is only a short walk from the station, and much closer than our house."

"What time would suit you best?"

"Shall we say midday, if you can make it by then."

"Thank you so much. I'll ring to confirm when I've checked the train times."

The line from Exeter to Waterloo was notoriously slow compared to the two hours the best service to Paddington offered. It did have the advantage, however, that Simon could catch the train at Whimple, one of the small stations between Exeter and Honiton, and not have to pay the exorbitant car park charges at Exeter's main St. David's station. However, thinking that it would be a useful opportunity to have another look at Malcolm's house unencumbered by the police, Simon decided to go by car.

Carshalton, at the end of the Wandle river trail from Wandsworth and down through Morden, was sufficiently distant from Greater London suburbia to still retain a village atmosphere - albeit a considerably enlarged village. Although Sarah had given him directions for walking from the station, he found the hostelry where they were to meet without any difficulty and was also fortunate enough to park in the street nearby. The Sun Inn had several customers but the lunchtime trade hadn't really started. It was just past midday when he arrived. One woman was sitting on her own, sipping a soft drink. Simon had no difficulty recognising her, although she looked younger than the fifty years that Malcolm had mentioned from the OnlyOne posting on the Flirty site.

"Sarah Manning?" he asked quietly, stepping up to her table. She looked up and nodded. "I'm Simon Cook. Thank you for agreeing to meet me."

She stood up and shook hands.

"Can I get you another?" Simon asked.

"Thank you. Another tonic water, please."

Simon ordered her drink and a half pint of bitter for himself.

"Your phone call intrigued me. I hope you can enlighten me as to what's going on."

"I will try to do so, Mrs Manning ... "

"Sarah, please."

"Okay, Sarah. First of all, I have a letter for you from Malcolm." He passed it over and waited while she opened the envelope.

"Thank you," said Sarah when she had finished reading the letter. "Please thank Malcolm also, and assure him that I would really like to meet him."

"I'll pass on your message. Now, I'd also like to show you a photograph." He took a copy of the photo of Tricia from his pocket and handed it over."

"That's me!" Sarah exclaimed in shock. "Where did you get it?"

"Just one more thing before I answer that. May I ask you pull back your blouse a little bit to the left? If this photograph is definitely of you and has not been edited then there should be a small mole just here." Simon touched his own shirt in the corresponding place.

"Yes, it is definitely me," Sarah said quietly, offering the proof.

"Good. I think that is going to prove pretty conclusively that Malcolm is being set up to take the blame for a crime he did not commit, subject to the answer to a question which I hope will not embarrass you. Have you ever posted anything on a dating site called Flirty?"

"No way! I've never heard of it. And let me remind you, I'm married, happily, with two kids!"

"Okay, that's what I thought. I'll start at the beginning. A few weeks ago, following an unsolicited advertising email, Malcolm signed up to what he thought was an on-line friendship site for widowers. It wasn't quite was he expected but he was attracted by a message from a woman calling herself OnlyOne – with a photograph that reminded him of your mother, Barbara. You do in fact look very much like your mother. The photograph was the one I have just shown you."

"But that's impossible!"

"Well, I'm not sure how it was done but I'm hoping that some ideas may come up as a result of this meeting. I would mention that there was also a very erotic photograph of the body of a naked woman, but we know that is was not the same person. There was no mole on that body."

"My god, I never thought that I'd have cause to be grateful for that small blemish on my skin!"

"Anyhow," Simon continued, "Malcolm and this woman - Tricia, was the name she gave - exchanged messages and he arranged to meet her in Exeter on a Saturday lunchtime. He drove down on the Friday, and sent her a text message on her phone to say he'd arrived in the city, and she replied, confirming the meeting. She never turned up but sent another message rearranging the meeting for the evening. Again she failed to appear!"

"Ok...ay," Sarah said cautiously, "so what happened then?"

"A woman's body was discovered - a much older woman - in the river. She had been killed and severely beaten about the face on the Saturday evening. Nearby a mobile was found with her prints and the exchange of texts with Malcolm."

Sarah put her hand to her mouth. "That's horrible and really bizarre. You don't think Malcolm did it?"

"I'm sure he didn't but the police think otherwise. Apparently he knew the victim at university. I was at Exeter at the same time as Malcolm and we were friends, though I didn't personally know her. From an analysis of Malcolm's computer, it seems likely that this dead woman was the one posing as Tricia. There is various circumstantial evidence, enough for the police to arrest and charge him. He's now being held at Exeter police station.

"Oh my God, the poor man!" Sarah cried. "What can you do? What can we do?"

"Your testimony is very important. It will prove that he was lured to Exeter, to be in the area when the crime was committed. Let's just consider the photograph again. It there any indication that you can see as to when or where it was taken?"

Sarah studied the picture closely for a couple of minutes. "That particular hairstyle, it's different to what I have now. I tried it for a short while, two or three weeks at the most, and didn't like it."

"When was that?"

"In the summer. July I think, though I could check in my diary."

"I'd be grateful for that. What about the location?"

"That's more tricky since it's mainly me and not much background." She looked again. "It's just possible - it could have been taken outside a house I was showing to a client. I'm an estate agent. There's just the suggestion of the top edge of one of our 'for sale' boards." She thought for a moment. "There was one guy I remember, had a camera with him, and insisted on taking several shots of the interior and the garden, 'to show to my daughter' he said, even though there were ample pictures available on line. This would have been around the same time, I think."

"That's very helpful, particularly as you don't appear to be looking at the camera," said Simon. "If you can dig out a date and a name that would be brilliant. By the way, what's the name of the estate agency you work for?"

"Scott Anderson. Bill Scott's my partner. We've just got a couple of offices, one in Mitcham which I look after, and one in Kingston that Bill handles."

"You're a partner?" Simon said in surprise, "And you've kept your maiden name?"

"I did start working for old Mr Scott before I was married. He retired a few years ago but kindly stood in for me when I took an extended holiday earlier this year. It just seemed sensible not to change my name for my business interests." Sarah knitted her forehead in thought. "Tell me, how would this person ... this person who has used my photo to trap Malcolm, how would he or she have known about me?"

"I'm not certain, but obviously he knew your mother was married to Malcolm, and that she had died..." Simon stopped. "Hang on a minute, you said 'he or she'. I know that the victim must have been involved in some way with this deception but she must have had some help to find your connection to Malcolm – something he didn't even know himself!"

"Hell hath no fury like a woman scorned," Sarah quoted the old saying

"Mmm. That is a good point. Now this person – I'm going to say 'he' for the moment – could have found out quite easily from public records when and where Barbara and Malcolm were married. Do you know whether your mother kept her Anderson married name when she left your father?"

"I think she did but I can't be certain."

"That should be easy enough to find out. And if she did then it would also be much easier to check if she had any children from her first marriage. And if he were really determined, the link to you at Scott Anderson might not have been too difficult. At some point he must have thought there would be a sufficient family likeness between you and your mother to use to his advantage."

"So what happens next?" Sarah asked, and then added, "I'm going to have to leave soon, I've got a client waiting for me at 2 pm."

"I've got some leads to follow up and if you can let me have any details concerning the photograph I may have enough to persuade the police that they need to look elsewhere, or, if the case does go to trial, enough to convince the jury that there is reasonable doubt."

"Okay. Thank you for your efforts, Simon."

"Will you stop for lunch?"

"No, I need to be going. But you carry on. The food here is good. And I look forward to meeting Malcolm when this has all been cleared up."

"He is looking forward to meeting you."

The pub was getting busier and the food that was being brought out looked very appetising. There seemed little point in seeking out somewhere else for lunch.

His mobile rang as he was about to leave. "Charlie!

Any news?"

"Yes, indeed. I think I have a name for our mysterious Tricia."

"Would that be Sarah Manning or Sarah Anderson by any chance?"

"What! You already know?" Charlie seemed crestfallen.

"I've just been talking to her. She's Barbara's long-lost daughter."

"But ... but how did you ...?"

"Sorry Charlie, you tell me how you got the name. It may prove very useful."

"I got a call at the office in response to the newspaper appeal. Some woman in ... hold on a sec ... in Mitcham. That's Surrey, I think. She was staying with a friend in Devon and saw a copy of the Express & Echo lying around. The woman told me she recognised the picture as the manager of an estate agent in the town."

"I can confirm that is correct."

"So how did Simon the supersleuth find out?"

"Nothing involving detective work at all. Malcolm's wife had written to her estranged daughter shortly before she died, seeking reconciliation. He recently received a reply from her

"Oh." Charlie felt deflated as his potential scoop of the year was trumped by a mundane exchange of correspondence.

"I'll fill you in when I get back," said Simon, "but in the meantime any information you can find about Richard Eastman's family might be useful. I've no direct line to any of them as far as I know. I'm heading off to Malcolm's house shortly. I'm not really expecting to find anything useful but you never know."

Simon had one more call to make.

"Exeter Police. Nicholls speaking."

"Hello, this is Simon Cook. Is your boss there?"

"He's out of the office at the moment. Should be back soon. Can I take a message?"

"Yes. Please tell him that I have identified the Tricia in the photograph, and have definite proof that the picture was taken and used without her permission. He can also get corroboration of the identity from the Express & Echo, who have had a response to the request for information they posted."

Chapter 18

Molly was just leaving the house with a bowl of dried cat food when a car pulled up by the pavement. With surprise, she recognised it immediately.

"Uncle Sean! What are you doing here so early?" she said as he climbed out.

"Ah, well, I had to deliver some urgently needed equipment for a client in town, and your Mum said you'd like some books you'd left behind. So thought I'd drop them off." He handed over a small plastic carrier bag.

Molly looked puzzled. "I think she must have misunderstood. I may have mentioned a couple of books I meant to bring but they certainly weren't essential. Never mind, thanks anyway. Here, hold this," she said, handing him the saucer, "while I put the bag indoors."

"Breakfast for someone's cat?" Sean asked, when she returned.

"Yes, our neighbour."

"Mind if I walk with you?" said Sean. "Need to stretch my legs a bit after the journey. Is your neighbour on holiday?"

"No, it's rather more serious than that?"

"Hospital then?"

"No, he's been arrested. The police were searching his house earlier this week."

"What's he supposed to have done?"

"I think he's accused of killing a woman in Exeter. Though I can't believe he would have done such a thing."

"You know him then?" Sean said innocently

"Yes, Dr Weston, from University. You were there when I mentioned to Mum that I thought I'd seen my former tutor near Uncle Barney's. That was when we were helping him move."

"I remember now. Just before your Grandad's funeral."

Molly happened to glance at Sean as she was talking. His face seemed to showing a satisfied grin and his head nodded up and down.

Her uncle opened the gate to Malcolm's drive, and stood back to let Molly through.

"Thank you."

Sean followed her round to the back door.

"That's strange," she said, "I must have used two saucers by mistake yesterday evening." She picked up the empty dishes and replaced them with the fresh bowl.

She gave a scream and stumbled backwards into her uncle's arms as the back door opened.

"What ...? Oh, sorry if I frightened you, Molly," said Simon. "Thank you for looking after Shylock. I'd forgotten that you'd be round this morning."

"What are you doing here?" Molly asked, "Have you any more news about Dr Weston?"

"Sorry again. I was talking to his stepdaughter up near London yesterday afternoon, and thought I'd just have a look round his house without the police breathing down my neck. I got here later than expected and decided to stay overnight." Simon turned an enquiring eye to Molly's companion, "I don't think we've met."

"I'm Molly's uncle, Sean." He paused for a moment, puckering his forehead as a worrying thought entered his mind. He held out his hand.

"Pleased to meet you."

"Molly has told me a bit about Malcolm. You're his friend?"

"Yes, and his lawyer as well, I'm afraid."

"So what's the likely outcome?"

"Difficult to say. The police have got good grounds for charging him but there are some unexplained issues that may be to his benefit if they can be resolved."

"Such as?"

"I'm sorry, Sean, I'm not at liberty to disclose such matters."

"I understand," Sean replied, trying to hide his disappointment at not learning more from this unexpected encounter.

"Will you be staying longer?" asked Molly. "Just wondered whether I'll need to feed Shylock this evening."

"I'll be heading back to Exeter sometime today. I really appreciate your care of Malcolm's cat."

"No problem." Molly and her uncle took their leave.

Sean seemed rather withdrawn. Far less chatty than when he had arrived.

"Any plans for the rest of the day, Uncle?"

"I had wondered if you and Barney might like a trip out into the country somewhere, but I think that I'll make my way home. There are some things I need to sort out."

"That's a shame." Molly, without her own transport, had little opportunity to explore the Sussex countryside, or even the urban sprawl westwards along the coast to Shoreham-by-Sea. It looked like being another warm sunny day in the Indian summer the country was enjoying. Her Uncle Barney, however, rarely ventured out further than the local pub on foot and although he had a car, the longest journey he made was for any shopping he couldn't get at the nearby convenience store.

"Perhaps next time," said Sean.

"I'd like that," said Molly. She knew it was quite possible that his job as a commercial traveller for an optical goods company in London could bring him to Brighton again at any time. His irregular hours as necessitated by his frequent journeys away from home also suited his single lifestyle. He had never married but still lived in the family home in Wimbledon with his recently widowed mother, or, rather, until recently when she had been admitted to a care home. Her mother, Sally, was his sister, and they lived quite close by in Putney.

After getting a small jar of Nescafe and some pastries for breakfast from the local convenience store, Simon settled down to the job of going through Malcolm's papers. There were documents he needed if he was going to handle his friend's financial affairs if he were imprisoned. Something was niggling in Simon's mind, however, and it was late morning before it clicked. Sean had without hesitation mentioned his friend's Christian name yet it didn't ring true that he had heard it from Molly, as he claimed. Perhaps from Barney?

Molly, too, was having some niggling thoughts. Her uncle, who had been quite bright and breezy on arrival, had seemed to become much more reticent and serious after their encounter with Simon. On an impulse she rang her mother.

"Hi there, love," Sally Pritchard answered, "It's not Sunday." The usual day for their weekly chat. "Everything all right?"

"Yes, Mum, I'm fine." She paused then said, "Uncle Sean was here today."

"Really? He didn't mention he was going to Brighton when I saw him yesterday. What did he want?"

"That's what's a bit odd. Said he was down in Brighton on business and he'd brought some books that you'd told him I needed. He said he was going to invite us both to take a trip into the country as he'd got the rest of the day free, but then changed his mind."

"Strange. I'd said, 'whenever' about the books. It's not often he works on a Saturday but not unknown. So why did you think it odd?"

"I don't know. He seemed to be more than casually curious about Dr Weston when we went there to feed the cat and Dr Weston's friend was staying there. He seemed to have a very strange reaction too when Granddad's funeral was mentioned."

"Did he mention it, or was it you?"

"He did."

Sally paused, choosing her words carefully. "Uncle Sean was very upset at your Grandad's death, and very angry. It's not been easy either with your Grandma. Even though she's got Alzheimer's it's obvious that she missed him. She's not very well at all, I'm afraid."

"Why was he angry?"

"When he was clearing out Dad's things after he died, he came across a diary. He showed it to me. It was horrible, the suffering and injustice Dad had felt and his hatred of the person he believed to be responsible."

"What do you mean?" Molly felt fearful of the reply.

"Grandad blamed Malcolm Weston for ruining his life. His hatred had obviously been festering for many years, so when I mentioned in passing that Dr Weston had been your tutor and you'd seen him recently near Uncle Barney's he became very agitated. I thought he was going to have a heart attack. It appears that the man who was the focus of his grievances resurfacing so close to his family after so many years was just too much for him to cope with. That's why he took his life.

"Oh my God," cried Molly, "I wish I hadn't said anything."

"You weren't to know love. Don't blame yourself."

"But what on earth had Dr Weston done to cause such distress?"

"There are things about your grandfather's past that we haven't told you. When you next come home I'll show you the diary, and you'll understand."

Chapter 19

"Any more information about Richard Eastman's family, Bob?" Matthews said as he hung up his coat and trilby on the hook on his office door.

"Nothing of significance, really. I imagine the family were pretty devastated by his suicide. Son is unmarried and lived at home with his parents. He's still there but mother has been moved to a home, as her Alzheimer's has been aggravated by the loss of her husband. Sister also lives in London, married, with a daughter now at university. Interestingly, at Sussex."

"Wonder if she knew Weston. What's her name?"

"Maureen Pritchard. Everyone calls her Molly." Nicholls flopped into the chair facing his boss across the desk, "You know, some things about this case are puzzling me."

"Such as? You're not the only one, Bob."

"Well, would Patty have walked to her death by the river? It suggests a car could be involved, but it's difficult access to the Port Royal pub for a car – a narrow road, and very limited parking. Similarly for where her body was found. We've nothing from Weston's vehicle that shows she was ever in it. So, did she know the driver? Or, why would she have got into a car with a stranger? Was she drugged in the car?"

"We've got no CCTV at crucial points there."

"Also why all this guff about Tricia on their phones and laptops?"

Matthews thought deeply. "Tricia isn't mentioned on that phone by name, nor does it show her photo. If Weston's lawyer is correct then Tricia doesn't exist but the photo is of Weston's stepdaughter? How the hell did Patty come by it?" He then added, "I'm still intrigued by the hammer plastered with Patty's fingerprints. Perhaps we should take up his solicitor's offer and look at the other ones he's collected."

"Great! So whoever's prints we find on the murder weapon we charge that person as at least being an accomplice in the murder? Though how the bloody hell Patty Gallagher got to handle it is a mystery. And if Patty was carrying out a scam and Weston found out it would be a strong motive for her murder. Christ, we could do with a Hercule Poirot on this case!"

Simon was surprised to get the call on his mobile from D.I. Matthews. Even more so when he was asked to supply the very fingerprints he'd already been denied the opportunity to match with those on the hammer.

"I do not have the original dish from which the prints were taken," he replied, "but I do have the copies. You realise, of course, that these would not as such be admissible as evidence?"

"Yes indeed," Matthews replied. "I'm not - at this stage - going to ask where the prints were found, but if any are a match for the hammer then of course I would have to insist that you provide that information. I suspect that you have found a way that Dr Weston could have acquired the weapon."

"I couldn't possibly comment on that hypothesis," Simon said, then added, "but I do have another item that may have a different set of prints that could match the hammer. However, I would have to ask you to arrange for one of your colleagues from the Sussex force to do the test." Simon wasn't sure whether Sean had handled the cat bowl but he had seen him hold the gate open for Molly.

"Mmm, not sure about that, but I'll see what can be done." Matthews replied.

"I would like to see Dr Weston again. I would remind you that you will soon either have to release him or formally charge him."

When he rang off, Simon noticed that he had a voice message, *'It's Sarah, Ring me back.'*

His return call was picked up immediately. "Hi, Simon here. You have some news for me?" he said hopefully.

"Yes, indeed. I have a name for the chap who took

photos at a house viewing. Richard Eastman."

"Can you remember what he looked like?"

"Not really, sort of average height, middle aged."

"Definitely not old?"

"No. Why?"

"If it's the Richard Eastman I know then he had died weeks beforehand, and he would have been about my age. I presume you don't believe in ghosts."

Sarah caught her breath. "But... why ....why would this chap have given a false name?"

"I think he was more interested in you than in the house. I suspect it was Richard's son but I'm surprised that he even mentioned the surname. Probably wasn't expecting anyone to make the connection."

"And what is the connection?"

"Richard Eastman was convicted of rape of a female student when they were both at university. The same woman whose body was found and for which Malcolm is being held on suspicion of her murder."

Chapter 20

My life is about to end.

But in truth my life came to end over forty years ago. My birthday party and all my hopes and ambitions killed. A young man with a bright future condemned to spend years a prison cell and made to suffer to scorn and revulsion of those whom I had regarded as friends. And when I gained my freedom I was placed for life on a sex offenders register. Harassed by the police every time any women within a hundred miles of my home reported sexual molestation, and made to account for every moment of my day. I now take great care to avoid being alone in the house or going anywhere unaccompanied, to no avail. My family also came under suspicion.

The party. It's as vivid as if it were yesterday. It was meant to be a celebration of a notable milestone in my life. I'd invited practically everyone I knew at uni and there were a few there that I hadn't. Tagging along on someone's else's arm. Patsy Tanner, for instance. She claimed Malcolm Weston had invited her but she seemed to give him little consideration. She was more interested in being the centre of the attention herself. I flirted a bit with her but I'd heard she had a reputation for being uninterested and a total cold fish when it came to real sex. I knew other girls that were not so reserved. Plenty of booze. I was merry but not rolling drunk. Not so others. Drugs too probably. I didn't supply any but I didn't discourage others from using. I saw Malcolm coming down the stairs, There was no real need for him to have been up there, We had a loo in the lobby beyond the kitchen. I think he left soon afterwards. Some had already gone, and I assumed that Patsy was one of them. I hadn't noticed her for some time. Well after 11 pm there were a couple of stragglers left. William, Stephen and I were beginning to clear up. My other flatmate, Charlie, was god knows where. Ready for bed. I made a last call at the bathroom. When I returned I was surprised to see Patsy lying on my bed. I went over to her to see if she was okay. She woke up and as soon as she saw me she started screaming. Screaming her head off and yelling at me. It was then I saw the blood. Stephen came rushing in to see what was up. He took one look and shouted, "You bastard!" He called the police. When they arrived Patsy was still screaming that I'd raped her. I didn't - I would never have had sex with a girl without her consent, but the police didn't believe me. There were specks of blood on my clothes from when I leaned over her. There was a condom missing from my pack on the floor. Yes, I did use them but not that evening.

They charged me with rape. When they interviewed those that had been at the party, Malcolm claimed he had not been upstairs. I saw him! Why would he have denied it unless he was the one who had raped her? She was supposed to be his girl friend. He must have got annoyed seeing her flirting with other men, and known that she wouldn't get into bed with him willingly anyway. Patsy had become unconscious through a mixture of drink and drugs - and they found some of the drugs in my house. They weren't mine. William and Stephen didn't believe me, and neither did Charlie when he returned to the house soon after the police had arrived. Those at the party were so spaced out that no-one would swear that I'd been downstairs all of the time.

The years in prison were hell. A sex offender is the target of all kinds of abuse from other prisoners, and the prison officers turn a blind eye. Through good behaviour I was released after serving just over half of the eight years. The glimmer of hope came when I met Becky, who was my probation officer. She believed my story and did her best to help me put the past behind me. She married me and gave me two lovely children, for whom I am forever grateful.

Though the memories never fully went away, I thought I had learned to live with it. Until it all came back to me when I found out that Malcolm Weston – Doctor bloody Malcolm Weston had been teaching my lovely *granddaughter at university. I didn't rape Patsy. I wanted someone to believe me. I wanted someone to get Weston to face up to his crime and his deceit. I tried to contact my former flat mates. Stephen I'd thought was my closest friend but he's dead. I got a brief, "Sorry can't help" from William and sod all from Charlie. And Patsy? Did she see who raped her? I can't contact her - I'd be accused of harassment all over again.*

I might have coped but for even worse news. Weston is living just a stone's throw from where my granddaughter will be lodging. She will be at risk from this cowardly bastard who let me take the blame for his own sick lust.

With my own darling Becky's agreement, I have kept all details of my past life from my children, but she is no longer in a state to comprehend much of the routine of her daily life. I can't bear the thought of living without her, and I hope my departure will not affect her greatly. I am truly sorry that my children and granddaughter may find my death difficult to bear - and my hitherto hidden life story even more so - but I cannot bear to carry on while knowing that an evil lying rapist lives in blissful retirement so close to Molly.

I can't forgive Malcolm Weston for what he did. But I also have little sympathy for Patsy Tanner who flouted herself so freely yet frustrated any man who sought to enjoy her charms.

May God forgive this sin I am about to commit.

Richard Eastman.

Molly had become paler and paler as she read though her grandfather's letter. "I ... I ... I don't know what to say..." she stammered. "Oh God!" She broke down in tears.

"There's nothing we can do, my love," said her mother. "Remember your grandfather for how you knew him as I shall do as my father - a kind and loving man." She put her arms around her daughter. "He and grandma could have told us but would it have done any good? We might have grown up feeling guilt, shame or whatever. Instead they both decided to put the past behind them."

"But if I hadn't gone to Sussex ..."

"You mustn't blame yourself, Molly. It's just one of those quirks of fate."

"Does Uncle Barney know?"

"I doubt it, and I see no reason that he be told."

"But I'm not sure that I want to live so close to Dr Weston if what grandad says is true – and he's also suspected of murder" Molly shook her head, "He seemed such a nice man."

"Let's see what happens If he's found guilty then you won't have to worry about having him as a neighbour. If he's cleared and returns home you don't have to have any contact with him, and anyway in a few months you'll be finished at Sussex anyway."

Molly nodded, "Love you, Mum."

Chapter 21

Information was coming in from various sources but for Matthews it seemed to raise more questions than it solved, and, significantly failed to provide any firm proof of Weston's involvement with Patty Gallagher's death. His prints were not found on the hammer. No incriminating emails or other messages were found on his laptop other than the Flirty exchanges that Matthews already knew about. The fingerprints supplied by Simon Cook from as yet undisclosed source were no match for those found on the hammer, and Matthews was more than a little miffed that, having gone through a lot of hassle to arrange for someone from Brighton police to examine Weston's front gate, the report came back that there were so many different prints that it was virtually impossible to make any positive identification.

Patty's laptop, however, had proved more interesting. She had undoubtedly set up both the PayGal and OnlyOne accounts on Flirty, and the anonymous email to Weston offering a link to the dating site had been traced back to her.

Nicholls found his boss in pensive mood.

"Just thought you'll like to know, I've found Billie Webster."

Matthews looked blankly at his sergeant.

"You know, sir, the WPC that helped Patty"

Matthews nodded, "Oh yes. And?"

"She's long retired from the force but still living locally, Topsham way. She's now in her fifties, divorced and living alone, but she's got a lovely little granddaughter. Quite a matronly person and ..."

"Bob, save me her life story. Did she provide any useful information about Patty?"

"Well, yes and no."

Matthews rolled his eyes.

"Patty had confided in her way back, and she knew

about her rape by Eastman. Something Patty had not ever told her husband, if we can believe him. They have kept in touch over the years, however, and occasionally she has stayed overnight, presumably after Frank Gallagher had lost his rag with her."

"When had Webster last seen her - or stayed over."

"Not since the summer. Apparently she was upset when she called, not by what Frank had done but a phone call she had received."

"Was she able to give more details?"

"Not really but Billie got the impression it was something that reawakened bad memories of the past."

"I don't know what to make of this, Bob." Matthews said. "It does seem as if Weston was telling the truth about expecting to meet with Tricia, and it's pretty clear he was being tricked by Patty, though lord knows why. I think we're going to have to release him"

"If he'd found out about the deception it would have given him a motive, wouldn't it?"

"Possibly, but I'm feeling we're looking for another explanation."

"Gallagher?"

"Perhaps. Now, I'd like your opinion of some emails exchanged between Patty and someone called Seaman over the past couple of months." Matthews turned the laptop screen towards Nicholls.

'Found her. Plan could work.' Seaman
'Good. Send pic. Will let you know if he bites. Paygal
'Always the alternative.' Seaman
'Less risk this way.' Paygal

Matthews scrolled down, "And then this one, sent a few days before she was killed."

'Hooked. All set up for Sat.' Paygal
'Need me?' Seaman
'We'll keep to plan.'

"Who's Seaman?" asked Nicholls

"Your thoughts first."

"Well, I would say it's pretty strong evidence that she

and this other fellow are setting up some kind of scam. No names mentioned but the timing of the most recent exchange surely can't be a coincidence."

"I agree. I have some suspicions about who Seaman might be. Do we have the names of Eastman's children?"

"I think so. I've got a note here somewhere."

"In the meantime I'm going to call Weston's solicitor to say that we will be releasing him without charge, but that he still remains a person of interest in our enquiries. I think Cook will probably persuade him to spend a few more days in Devon."

Matthews snatched up the handset as his desktop phone trilled. "Well, speak of the devil," he whispered to Nicholls, who handed him a slip of paper. "Mr Cook, what can I do for you?" he said pleasantly.

"I spoke to your sergeant recently and asked him to pass on the message that I have positively identified Tricia in the photo."

"Yes, he did tell me. And who is she?"

"She is Sarah Manning, nee Anderson. She is Weston's stepdaughter by his wife's first marriage. He has never met her and until a couple of days ago knew nothing about her. I have spoken to her and she was unaware that her photograph had been taken and used on the dating website. The naked body is of a different person."

"That is very interesting, and supports some recent discoveries we have made!"

"She thinks she knows who might have taken the photograph and when. Someone posing as client, gave his name as Richard Eastman, and took several pictures of the property they were viewing. She's an estate agent, by the way."

"So this would have been before Eastman's suicide?"

"No, some weeks later. I think it might have been Eastman's son,"

Matthews looked at the note his sergeant had given him. "Sean Eastman?"

Simon was taken aback.

"Hello," said Matthews, "are you still there?"

"Yes, sorry. You did say Sean?"

"Yes. Do you know him, then?"

"Bloody hell. Yes, I'm pretty certain I do, though I wasn't aware of his surname. You remember when you were searching Dr Weston's house, there was a neighbour nosing round – the one who was looking after the cat?"

"Go on."

"That was Barney. His niece, Molly is staying with him while at university. Dr Weston was one of Molly's tutors in her first year. I visited the house again and met Molly with her other uncle, Sean, who apparently was visiting from London."

"Thanks, that has been a great help. I was in fact about to ring you to say that we are releasing Dr Weston, so if you would like to call around this afternoon that would be good. We would prefer that he stays in the area for the time being as we cannot completely remove him yet from our list of suspects."

"That is good news. I am sure we can come to some arrangement."

"I wonder, sir," Nicholls said when the call was terminated, "if Seaman could be Sean Eastman? A convenient shorthand."

"Very good, Bob. I had thoughts along the same lines. We need to have a word with this Uncle Sean."

Chapter 22

"Christ, I'm pleased to see you, Simon," said Malcolm as he was brought into the interview room. "Thanks for getting me out of this place!

"We're not quite out of the woods yet, I'm afraid, though information that has come to me supports findings from Inspector Matthews here, and gives credibility to your claim of having been set up."

"We are looking at some other leads, now," Matthews followed, "although we can't rule you out as a suspect." Matthews looked at Simon as he added, "We would like you to remain in the area for the time being."

"That is okay with me," Simon said. "Malcolm?"

"I suppose. I would really like to get back home though."

Between them Matthews and Simon updated him on the developments, particularly on the identity of Tricia, and the exchange of messages between Sean Eastman and Patty Gallagher.

"Would you care to make any comments, Dr Weston." Matthews asked.

"You think that this whole business was triggered by Molly attending my lectures and subsequently lodging with her uncle, my neighbour Barney?"

"That seems to be the connection."

"But why?"

"We were hoping you might have some ideas on that."

Malcolm thought deeply for a few minutes. "I've not been in touch with either Richard Eastman or Patsy Tanner since they dropped out of university. Richard always maintained he was innocent of the rape. Perhaps he had suspicions about me and somehow persuaded Patsy that I had raped her."

"Did you?" Nicholls interjected.

"No! I've already told you I didn't - and I don't know who did if it wasn't Eastman."

"So what would have been the purpose of setting you up?"

"Revenge? Perhaps she planned to kill me."

"But you got to her first?" Nicholls again.

"No. Remember I didn't even know about her death until you identified her – and even then not until you gave her former name."

"Or maybe they wanted to set you up for a crime you didn't commit, rather like what Eastman believed had happened to him?" Matthews mused.

"Interesting thought, inspector. But you are not suggesting she killed herself so that Dr Weston would take the blame?" said Simon.

"Obviously something didn't work out quite as she had planned!" Matthews replied. "Anyhow, you are free to go now - and also, we have finished with your car."

"Full service and M.O.T. ?" said Malcolm.

"In your dreams!"

Outside, Malcolm took a deep breath. "God, I'm glad to be out in the free fresh air!"

"What do you want to do? Simon asked.

"A pint would be good. Is your local open? I'll collect my car and follow you back."

"Okay."

"Oh, wait a minute," said Malcolm, "I've got a message on my phone. It's only just been returned to me." He pressed the keypad. "It's from William. He wants to meet with me."

"Do you want me to come too?"

"As you wish. I don't expect he'd object." Malcolm said, while dialling.

Simon thought for a moment before replying, "No, you go on, if he's at home now. You've got your car. I'll see you back at my place."

"William Forth here."

"William, it's Malcolm. You asked me to call."

"Yes, I'm been trying to get in touch with you for the last two or three days. Are you still in Exeter?"

"I've been held at the police station. They've only just let me go"

"What! Why?"

"I'll fill you in when we meet. If you're free, I'll be with you in about ten minutes. Can we meet at The Lighter? I'm dying for a pint and I can park there easily."

"Fine, See you shortly."

Malcolm guessed by the time William had got ready and walked to the pub he would be arriving. Sure enough, as he was locking his car he saw William saunter round onto the quayside.

They took a seat outside. "Thanks for coming," said William, "You sounded desperate for a pint, so what can I get you? I'd recommend the Fursty Ferret or Hopping Hare if you prefer a pale ale. "

"I'll go for the Ferret."

William soon returned with two foaming pints.

"What was it you wanted to contact me about?" Malcolm asked, after he had given an account of developments since they had met the previous Sunday."

"From what you have just told me it seems even more relevant. I was vaguely aware that the police had found a woman's body in the river but it was only when they mentioned her name that I took notice. On one of my Sunday stand-in services I was in St. Thomas's Church when this woman came up to me and asked if I remembered her. She was vaguely familiar but I couldn't put a name to the face. 'I'm Patty Gallagher' she said, 'but you would have known me as Patsy Tanner'."

"When was this?"

"Oh, some time ago. Last year probably. Anyhow, to cut a long story short, she seemed happy to have someone to talk to whom she felt would respect her confidentiality. I got pretty much her life history, though I must say I was a little surprised that she had sought the comfort of God after the treatment she had received from her so-called religious parents. Her husband seemed basically a decent chap but on occasions when he lost his temper she would ring me and come over, basically to restore some peace of mind."

Malcolm frowned.

"If it's what you are thinking, Malcolm, no, there was never any sexual side to it. I'm ... er... not that way inclined."

"So, had something changed recently?" Malcolm asked, wondering where his friend's disclosure was leading.

"Yes, it had." William seemed to be deliberating about how much to disclose. "You remember I said that Richard's son, Sean, had contacted me, and wanted to apologise to Patsy. Against my better judgement, in retrospect, I phoned her to tell her of Richard's death and of Sean's desire to make amends. I passed on Sean's phone number and left it to her. A few days later, she came to me, obviously upset. I thought perhaps Frank, her husband, had gone too far. But apparently Sean, instead of just apologising for her father's crime, had told her that he firmly believed that someone else was responsible.

"Did he say who?"

"She didn't tell me, but she said that she had been very disturbed not only by the reawakening of memories of that terrible event but that she might have also caused the wrong person to have been sent to jail. She confessed to turning to drink and drugs again to help her sleep at night and forget the whole thing and she was afraid that her husband would find out." William looked at Simon in anguish. "I really shouldn't have given her Sean's number."

"I suspect he would have found her regardless, if he were really determined."

"Perhaps. But I think now I may have made a even bigger mistake. She wanted my help in contacting anyone I knew who was a student at Exeter and might have been at the party."

"What did you tell her?"

"I just gave her the names that no doubt Sean had got from his father anyway before he died – myself, Charlie, yourself and Stephen. Simon wasn't at the party and others I don't remember. I was fond of the booze in those days too.

I did tell Charlie but he didn't seem too concerned."

"It does seem for some reason that I became the focus of their revenge campaign." said Malcolm.

"Do you think I should pass this information on to the police?"

"Well, it would help me, but it might also get them looking at you as a suspect. You knew her, you knew part of what she was up to, and you know the area."

"I hadn't thought of that!"

"I'll leave you to make that decision," said Malcolm. "Another pint?"

"No, I'll pass, thanks." William looked as if he could do with some counselling. "And you are driving. You don't want any more attention from the police!"

"True."

Over supper, Simon listened thoughtfully to Malcolm's account of the meeting. Some disturbing possibilities had entered his mind.

Chapter 23

Since he arrived in the office, Matthews had been considering the best way to approach Sean Eastman. They could call unannounced at his London home but there was the distinct possibility that he might not be at home, while a phone call in advance might well arouse fear that he was himself under suspicion. On an impulse he dialled a number.

"Hi Simon. Des Matthews here. I wonder if you might be able to help. When you were last in Brighton, you mentioned you had seen Sean Eastman, although you didn't actually know his surname."

"Yes."

"Did you by any chance notice what kind of car he was driving?"

"God, let me think. Um, I wouldn't want to swear in court but I think there was a Ford Mondeo parked outside of Barney's house."

"Colour?"

"Light - silver, grey, white. And no, before you ask, I have no idea of the registration number."

"Now you also said that you think it must have been Sean Eastman who visited our photo girl, Tricia. What was her real name?"

"Sarah."

"Right. Could you ring her and ask if she remembers the car her client drove that day? It's a bit of a long shot but I think there is a possibility that Eastman could have been in Exeter when Patty was killed, and we could check CCTVs in the area."

"Will do. I'll get back to you."

Fortunately, Simon found her at her office, and explained what he wanted. He also took the opportunity to pass on the good news that her stepfather had been released from custody. He was able to ring Matthews back within a quarter of an hour.

"Simon Cook here. Sarah also recalls a white Mondeo but like me, took no notice of the registration."

"Okay, thanks. We've at least got something to go on." He turned to his sergeant. "Bob, I'd like you to organise a check on all CCTV footage from cameras around the River & Canal area, from the inner Ring Road, Topsham Road, Alphington Road and from Countess Wear to the swing bridge from, say, Saturday noon to midnight on the day of the murder. Give priority to the first two. Pick up any white or silver Ford Mondeo and check the registration number. I'm looking for a car registered to Sean Eastman."

"That's going to take a month of Sundays!" Nicholls protested.

"Well get some help and get onto it."

*****

Sean was feeling uncomfortable. He was expecting his niece to call at any moment. His sister had told him that Molly had seen the letter left by their father, and had been upset by the thought that she had unwittingly been the trigger for her grandfather's suicide.

The doorbell rang. Sean took a deep breath and answered it.

"Hello, Uncle," said Molly, in a neutral tone, unlike her usual cheery greeting.

"Come in. I've been expecting you." He led her into the lounge of his father's house that he had inherited. His sister had been left most of the investments and cash deposits in the bank.

Molly came straight to the point. "Uncle, I'd like to know whether you have had anything to do with the reason why the police arrested Dr Weston."

"He was suspected of a woman's murder, " Sean replied.

"I know that!" Molly retorted. "I also know that grandad was jailed for raping the woman many years ago, and claimed that Dr Weston was the real culprit."

Sean put his head in his hands, gathering his thoughts.

"I was very angry when I found out why Dad had killed himself. Angry that this Dr Weston had enjoyed a good life and was swanning around in retirement while Dad had suffered.And worried about you, knowing this person and now living so close to him. I wanted to protect my precious niece."

Molly blushed. "I appreciate that thought, Uncle. But I've never had any cause to be wary of Dr Weston. He always behaved as a gentleman with me and other female students at college, and since I've been staying with Uncle Barney, I haven't really seen much of him." Molly paused, before returning to her original query. "What did you do?"

"If he'd turned up on my doorstep when I'd read the letter, I would probably have throttled him. But I thought that it would be far more appropriate if he were to suffer the same fate as Dad by being convicted of a crime he didn't commit."

"So?"

"I managed to make contact with the woman who had accused him, and persuaded her that Dad was not her attacker."

"And Dr Weston was? I bet that went down well," Molly said sarcastically.

"She was upset, naturally, but like me, she wanted to put things right."

"How, exactly?"

"I knew through you that Weston was living in Brighton. We came up with a scheme to entice Weston to Exeter, and set him up as having appeared to assault her."

"Sounds very complicated."

"Well, yes, it did depend on a quite a few pieces of a jigsaw falling into place. If it had failed I may well have taken the direct action of kidnapping Weston and dealing with him."

"I'm glad you didn't!"

"No, and I probably wouldn't have wanted to lay myself open to criminal charges. This way, I'm not sure that we would have actually been committing any crime."

"But the woman ended up dead! What went wrong?"

"I don't know. Everything had been working out fine. Weston had taken the bait and come to Exeter hoping to meet a woman that reminded him of his wife ..."

"How?" Molly interrupted.

"Just leave that for the moment, okay?"

Molly grudgingly nodded her head.

"The plan was that Weston would be asked to meet this woman in the evening at this pub by the river. I'd observe him – he didn't know me. Patsy, that's the original victim, would be in a sheltered park area a short distance away. She would get her clothes dishevelled, nick her forehead and tap it gently with the hammer to get some blood on it and then call Weston for help, saying she'd been attacked. I would then follow him to where Patsy was, appear like concerned citizen,and rescue her by stunning Weston. We would make sure he got his prints on the hammer, which would be left nearby to be found. I would take Patsy by car and drop her off near the police station. She would have claimed her rescuer didn't want to leave his name."

"That sounds most ingenious. So what didn't happen as planned?"

"Weston never got the call. Patsy was supposed to ring him about a quarter to nine. He waited, oh, I suppose until about nine-fifteen or so then left, pretty well miffed. I went to the meeting place but there was no sign of Patsy - or the hammer."

"Didn't you try ringing her?"

"Yes, when I got back to my car. I'd left it quite close. There was no reply, and I didn't really want to leave a message."

"But Dr Weston has been charged with her murder. Surely you should tell the police. If you were watching him you know that he certainly didn't do it."

"There is nothing to connect me to Patsy. I don't want to compromise that situation by going to the police."

Molly looked long and hard at her uncle. "I don't know what to say. I'm not proud of what you've done, not happy at all."

"I did it to protect you!"

"Perhaps, but I think you could have just told me to be careful around Dr Weston."

"I hope you aren't going to say anything to the police. Please, Molly!"

She'd never heard her uncle pleading like that before, obviously worried. "No, I'm not. Just before I came round here I heard from Uncle Barney. He'd had a call from Dr Weston to say the police had released him without charge, though he was still staying Exeter for a few days."

Sean didn't look any more reassured

Chapter 24

Nicholls approached his boss with a sheaf of papers in his hand. "You wouldn't believe how many people in Exeter drive a Ford Mondeo!"

"Have you found anything else actually useful?" Matthews asked with a touch of sarcasm.

"Yes. Fortunately on the first route we checked – the Topsham Road. The other roads haven't been looked at yet. We clocked up twelve white, cream or silver Mondeos. One of them is registered to a Sean Eastman, with an address in Wimbledon."

"What time was this?"

We've got two sightings. One at about seven o'clock Saturday evening, southbound from the Inner By-Pass junction, and another, three hours later, also southbound towards the Countess Wear roundabout."

"Well done!" I don't think we need to check anywhere else at the moment but that puts Eastman definitely in the frame for the killing. Fancy a trip to London?"

"Fine. When?"

"I think we have enough to bring Eastman in for questioning. I'm going to have a word with someone I know at the Met. If we can get him at a local police station we'll talk to him there."

Next morning Matthews and Nicholls caught the fast train from Exeter to Paddington and were at Wandsworth Police Station by late morning for an interview, under caution, with Eastman. They had arranged for him to be arrested early that morning at his home before he set out for work, on suspicion of murder. He had time to arrange legal representation before being questioned.

Eastman was brought to the interview room accompanied by smartly dressed middle-aged woman who introduced herself as his solicitor.

"Good morning. I am Inspector Matthews from Devon and Cornwall Police, and this is my colleague, Sergeant

Nicholls. We are investigating the suspicious death of a woman in Exeter on Saturday, 16th October. Her name was Patty Gallagher."

"I don't know anyone by that name," Sean said brusquely.

"You may like to consider your answer," said Matthews. "We have evidence that you were in correspondence with her in the weeks prior to her death."

"Bloody bitch," Sean muttered. His solicitor looked at him sharply.

"I'm sorry, were you referring to Patty Gallagher?"

"No, my niece, Molly. She's got completely the wrong idea. She swore she wasn't going to tell the police."

"Tell us what, Mr Eastman? For your information we have no knowledge of Molly. She has not been in contact with us. Our information comes from other sources. But perhaps we ought to have a word with her."

"I'd rather you didn't involve her if what you say is true."

"I'm afraid we will have to be the judge of that, but if you co-operate with us, we may not need to bother her."

Sean nodded.

"Now, do you wish to change your statement that you didn't know Patty Gallagher?"

Sean looked at his lawyer before replying. "I knew her."

"Would you care to elaborate?"

"You probably know that my father was convicted of her rape - a charge which he always denied. He believed that another student at the time, Malcolm Weston, had done it, and let him take the blame, but of course, he couldn't prove it. He'd learnt to live with it and kept it secret from my sister and I until he committed suicide. A chance encounter had brought Weston unknowingly back into contact with the family. With that, and my mother's advancing Alzheimer's he just couldn't cope any more."

"So what did you do?"

"I wanted retribution. I wanted Weston to suffer as my father had. I found out where Patsy – or Patty, as she now called herself, was living." Sean continued to describe the trap he and Patty had devised.

"For the record, can you confirm that you took a photograph of Weston's stepdaughter, without her knowledge, and used it to entice Weston to Exeter?" Matthews asked.

"Yes. I'd learnt from Molly and Barney - I think you've met them, he's my sister's husband's brother - that Weston had recently lost his wife after their silver wedding anniversary. As a neighbour and, apparently, a drinking companion, Barney knew quite a lot about Weston, and through some casual probing, I found that his wife had been married before and had an estranged daughter whom Weston had never met. I did some checking and found that she'd had a daughter who was living not all that far away. I guess you know the rest."

When you were in contact with Patty, did you use an alias?"

"Yes."

"What was it?"

"Seaman."

"Thank you. We have found some exchanges between Patty, or Paygal, as she called herself, and Seaman. Now, turning to the weekend in question, were you in Exeter on Saturday 16th?

Sean paused, and looked at his solicitor, who gently shrugged her shoulders. "I'm not sure ... I travel at lot in my job, and I do get that way sometimes."

"Come now, Mr Eastman, it wasn't that long ago. And let me help you refresh your memory. Your car was recorded on the Saturday evening on two occasions on the Topsham road. Coincidentally that road is also close to the river where Patty's body was found that same evening."

Sean slumped in his chair. "Yes, I was there. I was driving my car."

"So can you tell us what happened?"

His solicitor intervened. "May I have a quick word in private with my client?"

"Of course. We'll take a short break. Say ten minutes?"

Matthews spoke to the recorder "Interview suspended at 11.45 am" and switched it off.

When they returned, the solicitor said, "My client is ready to make a full statement about the events that Saturday evening."

"Very well," said Matthews, "Please continue, Mr Eastman."

"I've already told you of the plan we had set up, and it seemed to be going well. I was a little worried that she might have her own agenda, possibly even planning to kill Weston. Then no call from Patty. Weston eventually left and started walking back toward the Quay. I went the other way to our agreed rendezvous but she wasn't there. No sign of her at all. I didn't know what to do. I felt that she had let me down."

"Go on."

"I left that park area and started heading back towards the road where I'd left my car. I noticed a small access point to the river – a small beach, I don't know, probably for anglers. I went down there. Patty was lying there, unconscious I thought at first, but when I went to shake her – wake her up – I realised she wasn't breathing. She was dead." Sean took a deep breath before continuing. "I was furious. Whatever she'd done, or whoever had killed her, she'd ruined my plans to implicate Weston. In frustration and anger I picked up a large stone and smashed it into her face several times. And threw the stone into the river,"

Matthews frowned. It was a confession but not what he was expecting.

"I swear I didn't kill her! She was already dead." Sean shouted in anguish.

"We need to discuss the implications of your account, Mr Eastman. We will return shortly."

Outside in the corridor, Nicholls said, "What do you make of that?"

"I don't know. It does tie in with the pathologist's report that she was dead before the serious facial injuries were inflicted."

"So who was responsible for her death? Eastman's evidence lets Weston off the hook. And if his account is true we can't charge him with murdering a corpse."

"Mmm. I'm not even sure myself about the legal position of attacking a dead body. Anyway, there are one or two more questions we need to ask him."

Sean and his solicitor stopped talking as soon as they heard the door open.

"Mr Eastman, we will need to look again carefully at the post mortem results to see if they support or contradict your statement, which I must say I find rather ... er....bizarre."

Nicholls posed the next question. "Did you put the body into the water?"

"Yes," he whispered.

"Why?"

"Christ, I don't know. I regretted what I'd done to Patty but realised that it could still work against Weston. I don't think anyone at the pub had spoken to him and I wasn't going to give him an alibi. I thought the body in the river might get washed downstream and give more time before it was discovered, And time for me to get away."

"Tell me," said Matthews, "Did you take any of Patty's things? A handbag, perhaps?"

"Yes, I took her bag. She didn't have her phone with her."

"Was there anything else in the bag/"

"Cards, usual women's stuff.

"Money?"

"A tenner and some loose change, that's all."

"Syringe?"

"No. Why should there be?"

"No matter. What did you do with the bag?

"I dumped it in a waste bin at Taunton Deane services. I stopped there for a coffee on my way home. What is going to happen to me now?"

"We need to check several aspects of your account but

at the moment you are free to go. We may bring charges against you for obstructing the course of justice. Until then or until we clear you completely I would like you to surrender your passport to the police here. We don't want you leaving the country."

"That wouldn't happen, I assure you."

Matthews and Nicholls had plenty of time for contemplation on the return journey to Exeter.

"So you believe his story, sir?"

"I'm not sure. I'm going to go through the pathologist's report with a fine tooth comb. At the moment the best we are looking at is a possible suicide and a vicious attack on a dead body. We need to conduct a detailed search around that beach area that Eastman mentioned. The body was actually found further downstream. The weir would have given the river enough momentum to move the body."

"It still begs the question of whether anyone else was involved. Why didn't she phone as planned? I can't see her just changing her mind after all that detailed planning."

"It's possible she may have dropped her phone without realising. I think we should ask for another examination of the hammer to see if it was only Patty's blood on it."

"What's your thinking there, sir?"

"The hammer wasn't found near Patty even though, according to Sean, she was going to have one with her. She may have been attacked by someone else and got in a damaging blow. And we still have a set of unidentified fingerprints."

Chapter 25

Malcolm was feeling much more relaxed after being a free man once again, even though he understood he was not definitely out of scrutiny by the police. He was looking forward to getting back home where he expected that Shylock would be glad to see him. He owed Barney a few drinks for feeding the cat ever since he'd been stuck in Exeter.

Simon had left the house after breakfast. Malcolm assumed he'd had some work to do at his office. He found Malcolm typing away at his laptop.

"Keeping busy?" said Simon when he returned near lunchtime and saw Malcolm pounding away at the keyboard.

"I'm writing to my new step-daughter again. I'm hoping that we can arrange to meet up again sometime soon."

"Good idea. Fancy a pint when you've finished?"

"I wouldn't say no. I've nearly finished here."

"Great. By the way, I've asked William and Charlie to join us later."

"Oh, any particular reason?"

"It thought it would be good for us to get together before you return to Brighton."

"I don't know when that will be!"

"I can update you on that. I'll tell you in the pub."

The Red Lion was fairly quiet and Simon opted for a table at the rear of the saloon.

With a couple of pints set out on the table in front of them Simon began, "Now, do you want the good or bad news first?"

"Cheer me up. Good news."

"I was asked to call at the police station on my way back from the office. They no longer regard you as a suspect. You are free to go home."

"What! Why? Oh, bloody hell, that is good news!" Malcolm nearly spilled his pint is disbelief.

"You have been given a cast iron alibi that means you had nothing to do with Patty's death?"

"By whom?"

"By Sean Eastman."

"What!" Malcolm could not believe his ears. "Why would he do that?"

Simon summarised the various points that the police had told him about Sean's statement..."

"Sean was quite adamant that he had been watching you at the Port Royal all evening, and that when you left, you headed back to the Quay."

"So he's been charged with her murder?"

"Well, no. He's admitted to battering her face with a stone but claimed she was already dead. The police have also confirmed that the facial injuries were mostly inflicted post mortem."

"Mostly post mortem?"

"There is some evidence that suggests she suffered a blow from a hammer prior to death but it certainly not enough to kill her, and possibly not even to stun her. And her blood was found on the hammer. Sean did give an explanation."

"That's incredible!" said Malcolm, after Simon had finished his account. "And I was the target?"

"Certainly, to get you wrongly arrested, for which they succeeded up to a point, but possibly for Patty to murder you."

Malcolm let out a deep breath. "So how did she die, if I didn't kill her and Sean didn't kill her."

"She probably took her own life. With an overdose of heroin. The police have found a hypodermic needle in the bushes near where Sean says he discovered her body. Not where the body was eventually found though, which is why they hadn't conducted a search in that place previously."

"But why?" asked Malcolm. He assumed this was the bad news that Simon had implied.

"I'm hoping that William and Charlie may be able to

help us understand. Ah, speak of the devil!"

William joined them at the table. "Malcolm's now a free man," said Simon.

"That's good to hear. Cheers!" William said, raising his glass.

"Tell me," said Simon, when William was seated, "From your meetings with Patty, would you have believed her capable of taking her own life?"

William considered the question for some time before replying. "Possibly. I wouldn't rule it out. She was pretty upset over the resurrection of memories of her student ordeal, and she wanted retribution."

"Would she have had access to heroin?"

"Almost certainly. I'm not sure how far she'd slipped back into drug abuse but she admitted that she had been using again."

It was just gone one o'clock when Charlie turned up. "Sorry, chaps. Got held up with some breaking news at work. Anyhow, good to see you all."

Although Malcolm had spoken to him on the phone, they hadn't met face to face during this visit. "Nasty bruise, you've got there, Charlie."

Charlie brushed his hand over his forehead, where on the left side there was a yellowish discoloured area around a healing scab. "I had an argument with a door. The door won."

Simon grimaced, "Nasty." he murmured. He refrained from further discussion of Patty's death until after they had eaten.

They chatted casually over their meal, bringing each other up to date on various happenings since they had last met, only touching on their student memories with Charlie's suggestion for his retirement party. "Yes I'm actually going to hand over the reins" he declared. Charlie, who had always been fond of a good pint, and a long-standing member of the local branch of CAMRA, was keen to reviving the old student custom of a pub crawl, but with a difference. "We've got four breweries within about five miles of each other," he said. "We'll start at the Topsham Brewery on the Quay, walk to the Exeter Brewery by the station, get the train to the Beer Engine pub and brewery at Newton St Cyres. Then a brisk walk to the main road for a short bus journey to Hanlon's brewery tap. We can get the bus back from there."

"I'm not sure about all that brisk walking," said Malcolm, "I'm not sure my bladder will cope with it!"

"Or we could do it the other way round," said Charlie. "Actually might work better. Bus to Hanlon's, bus to Newton St Cyres, then train back to Exeter and finish at the Quay. Anyhow you've got a few months to think about it."

"Now you mentioned the Quay, Charlie," said Simon, cautiously, "it reminds me that there are some things about what happened there the other week that still puzzle me. I thought we could put our heads together."

"Isn't that best left to the police," said Charlie.

"There are some things that they don't know about – at least, not yet."

"What do you mean?"

Simon brought Charlie up to date on the information that the three of them already had. "The big unanswered questions are why she appeared to have changed her mind and didn't call Sean, and why she took a fatal dose of heroin."

"I've no idea," said Charlie.

"I think you have," Simon said, seriously. "I'm sure that those unidentified fingerprints on the hammer are yours, and I would not be surprised to find your bloodstains on the hammer. It wasn't an argument with a door, was it? It was with Patty."

Malcolm and William both looked astonished at Simon's revelation.

"I don't like what you are suggesting," said Charlie. "I thought we were friends."

"Yes, we are," said Simon, "and that is why I'm asking you, as a friend, to clarify the situation. We have two people that we knew at college who have both committed suicide as the result of a tragic event that happened so many years ago. We have Malcolm, our friend here, who has been the target of a campaign at the very least to harm his reputation, if not his liberty and life. And we have a young man who had learned that the father he loved and respected may well have been wrongly convicted of a serious crime."

Charlie remained silent.

"For Christ's sake, Charlie, we need closure on this!" Simon was fast losing patience. "If you won't tell us, I swear to God I shall tell the police, regardless."

Charlie shot a baleful look at Simon. "Very well." He rested his arms on the table, and looked down, not wanting to meet any one of them in the eye. "I'd had an email from Richard Eastman way back after he'd heard that his granddaughter had come across Malcolm. I also had an email from Sean Eastman after his father died. I assumed, correctly I believe, that you too, William, had received similar communications."

"That's right." said William.

"I ignored the emails. I thought the matter was best left alone. However, when you mentioned that you had given some information about us to Patty and probably therefore to Sean, I became concerned. Particularly when you also said that they believed Malcolm was responsible."

"You didn't tell me that, William!" Malcolm interjected.

"I didn't want to worry you unnecessarily." William said meekly, "Sorry."

"So what did you do, Charlie," Simon said, to get him to continue.

"I suspected that they had got some scheme afoot but I didn't know what. But when Malcolm rang to say he was coming down for the weekend unexpectedly, I got worried."

"I thought you were away!" said Malcolm.

"No I wasn't, as such. But I didn't want you staying with me. I found out where Patty was living. I wanted to track her movements on that Saturday. I followed her to the Quay on Saturday lunchtime."

"She was there?"

"Yes. Of course, you weren't looking for her, you were looking for Tricia. And you would probably not have recognised her anyway. Anyhow, she watched you for a while and then left. I guess she wanted to make sure that you had turned up and she had got the right person. I was unsure whether to follow her or stay and keep an eye on you."

"Why didn't you come and say hello?"

"I thought about it. But I was still mystified as to what Patty's intentions were. When you left I followed you for a while and could see that you were going in the opposite direction to where Patty lived. As you know I phoned you, to see what you intended to do. I suspected that Patty would try to contact you again."

"Which she did."

"Yes, and you gave me the new rendezvous. Very interesting. It was after dark, along a quieter part of the river, and much closer to her house. I was convinced that whatever she was planning, it wasn't going to be good news for you."

Charlie took a long draught of his beer. "I knew the time and place of the meeting. I was pretty certain of the route Patty would take. I saw her come over the Trews Weir bridge. I was going to intercept her there but she went through the gate into the Belle Isles Park. I followed her and called her name - Patsy. She was startled and turned. I said gently, 'I'm Charlie. You may remember me. I was at the party.' She gasped as I said, 'I know that you are after Malcolm Weston.' She said, 'I'm going to end it' which I understood her to mean that she wanted to kill him. I told her she'd got the wrong man and that Malcolm was not responsible. I was not expecting what happened next. She yelled, 'It was you all the time!' and lunged at me with a hammer ...."

"Was it you?" Simon asked.

Charles continued, "She caught me on the side of the

head, and I fell to the ground. When I came round she had disappeared. She'd left the hammer and I took it and flung it in the river, or so I thought. I didn't know where she'd gone. I was bleeding, and my head hurt. I made my way back to my car."

The three others were silent, digesting what Charlie had told them.

At last Simon spoke up," Did you notice whether she was also bleeding? Her blood was found on the hammer."

Charlie thought for a moment. "It was dark, but, yes, I think she had a small cut on her face."

"Did she have her phone with her?" Malcolm asked.

"I don't know. I didn't see one."

""She could have dropped it when she ran off, I suppose," said William.

"Do you know who raped her?" Simon asked, "Was it you?"

"I was going to tell her. It was Stephen."

"Very convenient that he was killed in a car accident. He can't confirm or deny it."

"You surely don't think I did it?" Charlie said indignantly.

Simon shrugged his shoulders, "If Stephen didn't do it then either one of you is lying or there was someone else involved. Unless someone else makes a confession then there is no way anything can be proved to alter the original conviction."

"So what are you going to do?" Charlie asked Simon.

"I think it's more a question of what you are going to do. I think you need to tell the police what you have told us, and provide a blood and fingerprint sample. Since Sean has already confessed to smashing her face, and she has been shown to have overdosed there is no way they can bring charges against you. You can claim that you acted to protect Malcolm."

"That is true." said Charlie, "I did."

"William, you also ought to share your knowledge of Patsy's state of mind with the police. Again, it will not now be detrimental to Malcolm's case." Simon continued.

"I'll do that," William agreed .and then addressed Malcolm. "When are you going back home?"

"Tomorrow morning, I think. Thanks, Simon, for all the help you've given me, both professionally and as a friend."

"One more point," said William, "I presume Patsy's body will be released soon. Will you be coming back down for the funeral?"

Malcolm gave it some thought before replying, "Yes, I'd like to, if it's okay with her husband."

"I don't think it will be a problem. I'm hoping to speak with him anyway."

They were the only customers still in the pub, and the barmaid was hovering around, hoping that she could clear away their glasses and finish her shift.

Chapter 26

In the light of Charlie's disclosure about the perpetrator of the original assault on Patsy Tanner, William thought it would be appropriate to inform Sean Eastman, to hopefully remove the animosity that he still felt against Malcolm. He didn't know what further action, if any, the police might be taking against him now that Malcolm had been cleared of any involvement in Patsy's death.

He also wanted to speak to Frank Gallagher. He was undecided whether to phone in advance or just cold call and hope to find Frank Gallagher at home. He left it to the weekend and opted for the latter.

The Gallagher's house, in Cotfield Street, was just a stone's throw from the Exeter canal and quite easy access to the footpaths and cycle tracks along by the river. It would have been easy for Charlie to predict which route Patsy would have taken to meet Malcolm, and decide the best place to intercept her.

Gallagher answered the door. Probably as as a result of the loss of his wife, William thought, he appearance was quite dishevelled, unshaven, with unkempt long hair and stained singlet. Much the same impression he'd given to the police when they had first called. He noticed the dog collar and frowned. "Yes?" he said.

"Mr Gallagher? My name is William Forth – Reverend William Forth, as you've probably noticed. I knew your wife and I have come to offer my condolences."

Gallagher hesitated, and then stood back, "You'd better come in then."

"How did you know Patty?" Gallagher asked when William was seated.

"We met at St.Thomas Church. I was taking the service that day. Afterwards your wife came and introduced herself."

"Why?"

"She had recognised me. We were both students at

Exeter at the same time. I'm not sure how much you know about that period in her life."

"Nothing. She never told me."

"Do you want to know?"

"Doesn't really make any difference, now does it?"

"It might help you understand the pressure she had been under in recent weeks. You had noticed a change, I suspect."

"Yes, she seemed much more withdrawn, but she wouldn't tell me what was wrong. I had some suspicions, but ... well." Gallagher didn't elaborate, but held his head in his hands.

William paused, "I realise this is difficult. If you'd prefer....."

"No, go on. I need to know."

"Patty, or Patsy, as she was then known, was raped at a student party. A student, one of my flatmates, was charged and convicted. I had no reason to doubt that he was guilty. You know that her life fell apart after that and was only rebuilt when she met and married you."

Gallagher looked up and nodded.

"All would probably have been well but for a chance encounter that rekindled old memories and uncertainty. And, Mr Gallagher, I have to admit that I was unwittingly to blame for initiating the events that followed."

"What do you mean?" Gallagher asked sharply.

"I was contacted by the son of the convicted man after he had taken his own life. He genuinely seemed to want to apologise to the victim - your wife - for his father's actions. I gave Patty his phone number and left her to decide whether or not to take any action. Regrettably, she found that the man was more intent on revenge against the person whom his father had believed to be responsible for the crime. He persuaded Patty also to seek retribution."

"That might explain it." murmured Gallagher.

"I'm sorry, explain what?"

"I found some emails on her laptop. She'd left it open one day, the week before she died. Seemed to be she was cooking something up with this fellow Seaman, as he called himself. I thought she might even be preparing to leave me." Gallagher shuffled uncomfortably, "I didn't tell the police this but we had a blazing row that Saturday morning. I accused her of being unfaithful and plotting against me. She denied it vehemently and said I'd got it all wrong but she wouldn't tell me what had happened. I was so angry I lashed out at her..She fled the house, and the last thing she said was, 'All over, Frank, Soon be all over."

Frank Gallagher broke down. William, in all his time in holy orders, had never before seen such a strong man weeping real tears.

"It's all my fault. I shouldn't have hit her. It's my fault she's dead."

"You mustn't blame yourself for it all," William said gently, "She felt let down by so many men – by the student who assaulted her so long ago, by the man who used her for revenge, by myself, and by you at a critical time."

"Do you know now who was responsible for her ...her ...?"

"I think so. At the time I believed that the police had got the right person. Lately a friend who was also at the party told me that he now believed another housemate had done it. They are both dead."

"So we will never know for certain?"

William nodded. "Tell me, were you aware that Patty had started drinking and taking drugs again?"

"I had my suspicions but she never touched alcohol or anything else in my presence. She knew I would not approve, and would take it from her..."

"You've no idea where she got the drugs from?"

"Probably on this street. I know that the police have raided a house here in the past." Gallagher was getting back to normal, "Here, I haven't offered you a cuppa yet, I'm sorry."

"No problem. I'm just so sorry to have brought you further distress at this difficult time."

"No, I appreciate you coming. There are so many

things about Patty that I didn't know. But she was a good wife. I wish I'd been a better husband."

"Have you given any thought to the funeral arrangement?"

"Not really. Crematorium I suppose."

"I would be happy to take the service there, if you wish. Or make other arrangements. "

"Would you? I don't really want to have to think about it more than necessary."

Chapter 27

Malcolm was pleased to get back home and back to his normal life style. He vowed never to be tempted again by any on-line sites offering friendship, or more.

The reprise of another visit to Exeter for Patsy's funeral had, despite the sadness of the actual occasion and the circumstances of her death, had been more relaxing than his previous visit. Patsy's husband, whom he'd met for the first time, had seemed to be bearing up well, and William had given a very moving eulogy of her life, with minimal and non-controversial reference to her ordeals. Her friends from her craft group, Billie Webster, Inspector Matthews and a few neighbours had made up the rest of the small group of mourners. No other family members had been present. After the service Billie had invited everybody back to her place in Topsham for light refreshments. Malcolm and his three fellow Exeter alumni had felt it would be more appropriate to decline, to avoid any more stirring up of unhappy memories. They had taken the opportunity, instead, to do a trial run of Charlie's planned retirement brewery crawl. Charlie had told them that the police had confirmed that his blood and fingerprints had been found on the hammer, in corroboration of the statement he had volunteered.

Malcolm had set off from Simon's house late morning, neither of them having risen early after the previous evening's drinking. He'd driven leisurely, and it was late afternoon when he arrived home. Shylock greeted him, purring and rubbing against his legs before heading meaningfully towards the kitchen with a hopeful miaow.

He fed Shylock, made himself a mug of coffee and settled down in an armchair to sort through his mail. He recognised the handwriting on one envelope.

Dear Malcolm,

Thank you so much for your letter. I was so relieved to hear that you are free from all police investigations. It has been a trying time for you and I'm sorry that I unwittingly became involved in the deception that was inflicted upon you.

I would be delighted to accept your offer to visit you in Brighton, and we will arrange some time that is mutually convenient, perhaps in the New Year.

Since my mother died you will I suppose be on your own at Christmas. It would be lovely if you could come and spend the festive season with us. My children are looking forward to having another granddad!.

Love and best wishes,
Sarah.

Malcolm felt a tear in his eye. He wished that his loving wife could be with him to meet her daughter that she had barely known for over twenty five years.

As he sat there contemplating the twists of fate, he heard a knock on the door.

"Malcolm!" said Barney, "I saw your car outside. Good to have you back."

"Thanks, Barney, for caring for Shylock. Would you like to come in?"

"No, no, I was just wondering whether you'd like to join us for supper? I'm sure you haven't got anything in the house prepared."

"Er, no I haven't. I'd have probably popped down the pub. But yes, thanks, I'd like that."

"Just one thing, Malcolm. Molly will be there and also her Uncle Sean. Are you happy with that?"

Malcolm felt mixed emotions, "Er, I'm ..."

"No need to worry. It will be very amicable. He knows I was intending to invite you."

"Very well."

"Oh, by the way, when you see your friend, Simon, tell him I've found the hammer he was asking about. It had slipped down behind some boxes in the garage."

Malcolm restrained from making a disparaging comment. If Barney had searched more diligently at the outset it might have saved a lot of hassle. "Will do," he said simply.

"See you at seven o'clock then."

It was with some trepidation, nevertheless, that Malcolm arrived at Barney's front door, carrying a couple of bottles of Merlot he'd bought as a token of thanks for Barney's cat care.

"Hello again, Dr Weston," Molly greeted him.

"Malcolm, please. We can dispense with the formalities."

"And this is my Uncle Sean."

Malcolm looked at him, trying to judge from his expressionless face what his reaction would be. Malcolm offered his hand.

Sean responded with a firm handshake, "Only a week ago, this is one thing I would not have expected to have been doing."

"I can honestly say that meeting socially with you was not on my wish list either," Malcom replied. "However, without your statement to the police, which confirmed my account, I might still be under suspicion."

Sean grimaced and paused, considering his words carefully. "I now know that you were not in any way responsible for what happened to my father or to Patsy Tanner." He paused again, "I'm sorry for all the grief I've caused you over these past few weeks."

"Thank you," said Malcolm, "It's been a very traumatic time for both of us. Tell me, did the police take any action against you?"

"They weren't sure what to charge me with. I don't think they had ever come across a situation like that before. They believe Patsy had killed herself. In the end, they brought some nebulous charge of interfering with a police investigation. With my solicitor's help and admitting the offence, I was given a two year suspended sentence. So here I am, free, as long as I don't do it again."

"I think we should all put these events behind us now." said Malcolm.

"And enjoy the rest of the evening," said Barney.

Chapter 28

Something had been bugging Matthews ever since Charlie Coombes had presented himself at the police station and offered an explanation of why his blood and fingerprints were on the hammer. Although his story accounted for the suicide that was recorded on Patty's death certificate and, as such, the case was officially regarded as closed, Matthews had an uncomfortable feeling that he had missed a vital point.

He carefully read through all the statements from the various people he had interviewed and once again examined the pathologist's report. He almost missed a seemingly trivial detail.

He looked up a mobile number in the records.

"Mr Gallagher? This is Inspector Matthews. I'm sorry to bother you but I'd just like to clear up something which may be relevant to your wife's death."

"Is this necessary? I'm still trying to come to terms with her suicide."

"Just one question. Was Patty right or left handed?"

"Right." Gallagher sounded puzzled, "but what has that got to do with anything?"

"It may not be important but may help to tie up a loose end. Thank you." Matthews put the phone down and sat at his desk, deep in thought for a couple of minutes, then called in his sergeant.

Yes sir?"

"Bob, I'd like to run something past you, concerning Patty Gallagher's suicide

"Okay."

"The pathologist's report shows evidence of an injection in her right arm."

"So?"

"She was right-handed."

Nicholls knitted his brow, trying to see the relevance. At last he made the connection. "One would have therefore expected her to inject herself in the left arm."

"Precisely. And Coombes had a bruise on the left side of his head, consistent with a blow from a right-handed person facing him."

"Are you suggesting, sir, that her death may not have been suicide? That the heroin may have been deliberately injected by someone else?"

Matthews nodded.

"Like Coombes or Eastman?

Matthews nodded again.

"But you are definitely ruling out Weston?"

"I can't see any way that he could have been involved in the light of Eastman's statement."

"What do you think happened?"

"It's possible Eastman was responsible but I think it unlikely, having already confessed to inflicting facial damage post mortem. We only have Coombes' word for what happened when he confronted Patty. I think he wasn't rendered unconscious by the hammer blow, and probably wrested it from her grasp. She ran off, pursued by Coombes, to that beach where Eastman claimed to have found her body. He struck her down with the hammer. He searched her bag for her phone, saw the syringe and dope, and took advantage of it to inject her. He may not have intended to give her a lethal dose but give himself enough time to get well clear."

"Why would she have had the heroin with her?"

"Perhaps she did intend to kill herself after dealing with Weston?"

"So what happens now?"

"This is all speculation and, without any witnesses or confession, virtually impossible to prove. There were no other finger prints on the syringe, so he could have wiped it and then put it to Patty's hand."

"There is one other possible suspect, sir." Nicholls said tentatively.

"Oh, who's that?"

"William Forth. He was also at the student party, he

knew Patty in her new life, knew of her drug habits, and knows the area."

"Hmm, possible, I suppose, though it would have made that riverside area quite congested, with victim and four interested parties!" Matthews shrugged his shoulders. "I think we need to make a call or two.

Author's Note

My previous novel (Interface) began with a live on-line scene that was created to entice the viewer to make a journey that would put him at risk. I started thinking whether a doctored photograph and fictitious personal description on a dating site could similarly be used to lure someone unwittingly into a life-changing situation. When I came up with an idea why anyone would wish to construct such a scenario I felt I had the basis for a novel. Admittedly, for the deception to work for the perpetrator a number of links needed to fall into place but if that didn't happen a far less subtle alternative action was available.

The main action is set in the present day. However I decided that including any reference to covid restrictions was unnecessary, since none of the activities described would have been prevented by regulations in place at the time of writing.

The scene on the front page is Exeter Quay, looking towards the Prospect Inn.

I should like to thank Anne Bendix, Jeremy Child, and Carol Davies for their vigilance and comments in proof-reading, and for the team at New Generation for transforming the manuscript into a published book.

Apologies - In the final proof sent to me for approval I failed to notice that the Epilogue & Author's Note pages had inadvertently been interchanged.   Colin Andrews

Epilogue

That party. He'd survived the police scrutiny of those that had attended. He'd blocked any feelings of conscience over the shocking events of that evening, which had ruined the lives of two promising students. He knew the victim had suffered cruelly not only through the assault but from her total rejection by her parents who had blamed her for getting herself in the situation on the first place. Her alleged attacker, who always denied being responsible, had found his university education summarily curtailed when he was found guilty and sentenced to spend years in jail.

A long time ago. Only one other person had subsequently raised his suspicions about the verdict, and his voice had been silenced. Memories were long buried. Even the two most directly affected had eventually rebuilt their life, and both had found support in marriage.

But through a quirk of fate, the innocent conjunction of the lives of two people, one aged, one young, had resurrected old suspicions and resentment. He had no concern that any proof of his involvement would ever be found, but gossip and speculation could have seriously damaged his image as a worthy pillar of society. He had been prepared to do whatever was necessary to end the matter once and for all, but events had unfolded in such a way that he had been able to divert any suspicion without putting himself at risk

He could close the book and look forward to his retirement in a few months time without further threat.

A knock on the door awoke him from his reverie.

Lightning Source UK Ltd.
Milton Keynes UK
UKHW011820200722
406135UK00002B/565